THE RESURRECTED MAN

After abandoning his ship, space pilot Captain Baron dies in space, his body frozen and perfectly preserved. Five years later, doctors Le Maitre and Whitney, restore him to life using an experimental surgical technique. However, returning to Earth, Baron realises that now being legally dead, his only asset is the novelty of being a Resurrected Man. And, being ruthlessly exploited as such, he commits murder — but Inspector McMillan and his team discover that Baron is no longer quite human . . .

E. C. TUBB

THE RESURRECTED MAN

Complete and Unabridged

LINFORD
Leicester

First published in Great Britain

First Linford Edition
published 2008

British Library CIP Data

Tubb, E. C.
    The resurrected man.—Large print ed.—
Linford mystery library
    1. Astronauts—Fiction 2. Resuscitation—
Fiction 3. Murder—Investigation—Fiction
    4. Detective and mystery stories
    5. Large type books
    I. Title
    823.9'14 [F]

    ISBN 978–1–84782–493–6

Published by
F. A. Thorpe (Publishing)
Anstey, Leicestershire

Set by Words & Graphics Ltd.
Anstey, Leicestershire
Printed and bound in Great Britain by
T. J. International Ltd., Padstow, Cornwall

This book is printed on acid-free paper

1

Death was a tin can drifting in the void five million miles from Mars. A sleek hull studded with venturis and stuffed with torpedoes, filled with instruments and heavy multiple cannon. A man-made wasp of space, able to jerk into tremendous velocity, to strike and destroy, to run, to strike again. A tiny patrol ship of the Terran Fleet, its hull darkened against reflection, unarmoured, depending on speed and manoeuvrability for safety. It drifted in a silent orbit around the red planet, ready to smash any vessel attempting to run the blockade, and around it the invisible fingers of radar detectors swept space for a million miles.

The control room was a coffin. A tiny area in which two men lived and slept, breathed and ate, waited and watched. They were as much part of the ship as the instruments were, strapped in high acceleration padding and chafed by the harsh fabric and metal of spacesuits. Their food was capsules from a box, essential vitamins and drugs, for little energy food was needed during the long periods of free fall, and glucose provided all the energy they needed. Their water was rationed in ounces, reclaimed from waste and the humidity of the air, and they breathed almost pure oxygen at eight pounds pressure.

Two of them. Carlos the gunner, a Latin-American with liquid brown eyes, swarthy skin, and a palate for heavily spiced foods. His mind was a computer, his fingers part of his guns, his eyes blank from watching destruction. To him death was an abstract, ripped metal and blossoming flame, tiny scraps of raw humanity spinning in the void, the whine and throb of multiple cannon and the hissing discharge of homing torpedoes. A slight man with muscles of whipcord and rubber, steel and high-tension wire. A calm man who had long ago locked his private life in a rear compartment of his mind.

Baron was the captain. Tall and with

cropped black hair hugging his skull. Hard eyes of slate grey stared from either side of a hooked nose and his mouth was a tight gash over a jutting chin. A scar writhed over his left cheek, a jagged tracery of a time when searing metal had caressed him with a torrid kiss, and his brows rested like a thick bar over the cold bleakness of his eyes.

For a month now they had been cooped up in the too-small control room. For two more weeks they would have to live within the confines of their protective clothing. Then they would be relieved and return to the mother ship. They would be cleaned and their ship serviced and for a week they would relax, eating as men should eat, enjoy the tug of synthetic gravity and move free of the padding and pressure. Six weeks and a week off. Time after time until it had grown to be a routine, a habit pattern. Six weeks of high tension, of watching and waiting, ready to strike and run, to dodge and veer, to kill or be killed. Six weeks of hell and a week of life.

The glory of interplanetary war.

Baron thought about it as he sat, eyes automatically staring at the blank face of the radar screen. Below him, within arm's length, Carlos grunted as he jerked from a light doze, and yawned with a flash of white teeth.

'Time to eat?'

'Eat what, pills?' Baron shrugged, the movement hardly noticeable beneath his suit. 'Wait until we get relieved before you talk of eating.'

'Then I will eat,' promised Carlos. He reached for the inevitable gum and chewed silently for a moment, trying to fool his stomach with the released saliva. 'Tortillas,' he murmured. 'Chili and tamales, curries, so hot they skin the mouth — and wine. Ah, the wine!' He kissed the tips of his fingers. 'Chianti I think, and perhaps some of that sherry from Spain, the good sherry with the taste of almonds and the body of a saint. Tequila, of course, lots of tequila, and a steak, seared on the outside and raw within.' He grinned at the captain. 'Yes?'

'Stop teasing yourself.' Baron slumped back in the padded acceleration chair that served both as control seat and bed.

'You've two more weeks to go before you can stuff yourself and thinking about it only makes it harder.'

'A man can dream,' said Carlos with simple dignity. 'Even in space a man can dream.'

'Dream?' Baron gave a snort, half-laugh, half-contempt.

'I don't dream.'

'You should, my friend. This,' Carlos gestured with a gloved hand, 'this is but a part of life, the hard, cold reality, but in dreams a man can escape. He can eat and taste the tang of wine, the soft velvet of good liquor and even listen to the guitars at fiesta time. It is not good for a man not to dream.'

'No? Then why are you here, Carlos? Why do what you do if your heart isn't in it?'

'Did I say that?' White teeth flashed in a smile and liquid brown eyes glittered in merriment. 'I do what I have to do, the same as any other man, but that is not all my life. I shoot and kill and blast men to shatters but there is no emotion in it for me. No. I save that for the real things, the enjoyment of the body and the mind. I save the thrill for the wind in the evening and the song of birds, the thrum of guitars and the smiles of the dancing girls. They are the real things, my friend. They are the only things.'

'You're a fool,' said Baron, but he said it without heat. 'This is the reality.' He struck the edge of the control panel 'This.'

'And yet, when the war is over and we are back on Earth, when we can eat three times a day and walk without suits. Will this then not seem like a dream? Is it then more real than the other things? For then we will enjoy what we now dream of, and I do not think that I shall ever dream of what we do now.'

'The war will never end,' said Baron. He said it as if repeating a lesson, without emotion or conviction, mouthing the words as if they were a cold statement of fact. Carlos laughed.

'All things end, my friend, and this war will end as other wars have ended.' He hunched himself higher from the low-slung gunner's seat. 'I heard a whisper the last time we rested in the mother ship. A truce has been arranged and an armistice is a certainty. The Martian colonists are beaten, they know it, and we would be glad to end the war.' He smacked his lips. 'This may be the very last time we share this vigil together.'

'No.'

'Why not? We have won the war.'

'No!' Baron glared at the smiling face of the gunner. 'It will never end.'

'That is foolish,' said Carlos gently. 'Could it be that you don't want it to end?'

'I don't know.' The captain shook his head as if trying to clear it of cobwebs. 'I want peace, I suppose, but . . . '

'But you don't know what peace is.' Carlos nodded and his eyes held a surprising gentleness. 'You were trained for space, were you not? A pilot?'

'Yes.' Baron clenched his gloved hands and stared bleakly at the ranked instrument dials. 'I entered the Space Academy when I was fifteen, a ward of the State. Both my parents died in the Luna crash and they found me a place as compensation. I did five years' preliminary training before war was declared against Mars, and since then I've piloted a patrol ship.' He swallowed. 'That was ten years ago.'

Carlos nodded. He knew of the spartan discipline of the Space Academy, the rigorous training and deliberate crushing of softness and gentleness in those who were chosen to pilot the vessels of the space lanes. The Terran Fleet had room only for the best, and their standards were high. As a gunner Carlos was lucky. He was trained, of course, but a gunner's training was nothing as severe as that of a pilot. He could remember the ease of a world at peace and he had carefully kept the stringency of war divorced from his normal self. His soul was free from iron and he could shake off the past ten years as a dog shakes itself free of water.

Baron couldn't.

He had no other standards. He had only known war and the exigencies of war, the hair-trigger tension and harsh rigour of active service. Incredible as it seemed the captain was almost afraid of peace! Afraid of it as he could never be afraid of war. Carlos sighed and reached

8

for a fresh pack of gum.

'You will learn,' he said quietly. 'You will forget the steel and the guns, the night of space lit by distant stars and the gushing blood from strained capillaries. You will move more freely out of uniform, unhampered by metal and plastic, letting your limbs swing free and filling your lungs with God's sweet air. You will learn.'

'They will still need pilots,' said Baron grimly. 'With the war over trade will increase and men will be needed to steer the ships.'

'Yes?'

'Yes.' The captain sounded desperately hopeful. 'Space is my life, I know nothing else, and they will still need men.'

'So they will, my friend, but have they not men?' Carlos stared sombrely at the cold metal of the guns, winking in the soft illumination. 'Young men.'

'I am not old.'

'You are thirty, battle-scarred and overstrained, a man of war, a machine. There are others, younger men, higher officers, more suited perhaps to civilian life.'

'I am trained.'

'So are a thousand others, ten thousand others, maybe more. Will there be ships for all those men?'

'I don't know.' Sweat shone on the captain's harsh features. 'I've given my life to the Fleet, they will look after their own.'

'A comforting philosophy,' said the gunner quietly. 'I admire your faith.'

He yawned and stretched and hummed a snatch of some Latin rhythm, quick and blood-stirring, warm with the southern sun and redolent of lovers and wine, of gaiety and carefree indifference. Baron stared before him, not listening, his mind a cold mass of tissue, emotionless, calculating, indifferent to the lilt of tunes he had never heard and hearing could not understand.

A buzzer jarred the air with its harsh warning and a flood of ruby light replaced the soft glow. Again the grating warning, stilling the lilting song on the gunner's lips and turning the captain's mouth to a down-curved gash.

'Where?' Carlos strained forward as he

tried to see the radar screen, his backswung helmet clanging as it struck the metal of the hull. 'Many?'

'One.' Baron cut the alarm with a sweep of his palm and spun the knurled controls of the instruments. 'Coming out of the sun and heading for Mars.' He let his slate-eyes flicker over the bank of dials. 'Heading this way — fast.'

'Range?'

'Too far.' Baron grunted as the alarm shrilled again with calculated, nerve-scraping sound and green pips crawled over the surface of the radar screen. 'More of them! It must be a convoy.'

'Convoy?' Carlos frowned. 'That doesn't make sense. What do they hope to gain?'

'I know what they're going to get.' The captain tensed as he watched the flickering needles on the instrument panel. 'Five of them.' He grinned again, a twisting of his lips, a grimace utterly without humour. 'We're in luck. They'll pass through our sector. Stand by now.'

Carefully they swung down their helmets, sealed them, tested the inter-suit radios and settled in position on the radar screen the green flecks grew as the speeding ships drew nearer, and gyroscopes whined as Baron fed them power, turning the nose of the tiny ship by reverse torque.

'Ready?'

'Yes.'

'Fire a torpedo on the word.' Silence fell as he watched the swinging hand of the chronometer. 'Now!' Air hissed as a slender torpedo streaked into space, driven by a blast of compressed air. It spat away from the patrol ship, the delicate mechanism in its nose guiding it by mass-attraction towards the advancing ship.

'Now!'

A second torpedo, loaded with explosives and shrapnel to penetrate and riddle the enemy vessel with jagged death.

'Now!'

Again the slender shapes streaked from the belly of the ship, the hiss of the driving air echoing softly through the silent ship. Again and again until the bays were empty and the invisible containers of destruction had been sent on their way.

'Think that they will do any good?'

'Not unless those pilots are fools.' Baron rested his hands on the firing controls. 'If they're watching their radar they'll spot them but it will give them something to worry about.'

'Any answer yet?'

'I'm watching.' The captain narrowed his eyes as green flecks spotted the screen. 'Here they come.'

'Shall I blast them?'

'Don't be a fool! Time enough for target practice when you've got something decent in your sights. Ready now stand by for blast.'

'Ready.'

'Now!' Thunder drummed through the vessel as long streamers of blue-white flame spouted from the rear venturis. Weight slammed against them, driving them deep into the pneumatic padding of the acceleration chairs, and hull plates and metal structures protested with metallic whisperings as the powerful thrust of the rocket tubes jerked the ship from relative standstill into seven-gravity acceleration.

On the radar screen green flecks swelled and grew to skittering blobs and Carlos smiled with sheer happiness as he settled himself behind the smooth metal of his guns This was the time he enjoyed, not for the killing, he never thought of that, but for the sheer love of action and the testing of his skill. There was nothing for him to do but to snatch his opportunities and send streams of explosive shells towards the enemy ships. An automatic servo-mechanism could have done it as well, better even, for it could have tracked the ships and computed their probable position after time-lag. But a computer couldn't stand watch, take over if the captain fell sick, provide conversation and company. A computer was more expensive, and needed more servicing. Gunners were expendable.

Baron had a harder task. He had to pilot the ship, dodge homing torpedoes, approach within firing range, give the gunner opportunities to blast the enemy, and avoid answering fire. He had to do all this while travelling at high speeds and constantly altering accelerations. He had to watch his instruments, compute flight patterns, gauge distance, remain conscious and remain one jump ahead of enemy pilots who had all his qualifications and motives.

A pilot was considered old at twenty-eight and ready for reclassification at thirty. The jerking acceleration ruptured blood cells and capillaries, strained ligaments and tore muscles. The results were similar to those suffered by careless boxers after repeated blows on the head and punch-drunkenness was an occupational disease.

But now there was no time to think of that.

Visiscreens flickered into life as electrical silence was abandoned with the betraying lances of flame from the streaming rocket tubes. Radar had revealed their position but any meteor or drifting mass would have produced the same result on the screens. Once the rockets flared into life however, there could be no hope of concealment and Baron drew hard on the controls as he blasted towards the enemy ships.

A squat hulled cargo-type vessel swelled on the visiscreen fire sparking from the multiple cannon in its turret and streamers of flame slashing across the void from its steering jets. Carlos chuckled as he sighted it.

'Look at that fat pig. Watch.' His guns throbbed as he sent a stream of shells towards the ungainly vessel, Baron holding their course to give him a clear target, then blood gushed from ears and nose as he fed power to the steering jets and jerked the patrol ship from its line of sight. Struts groaned as the opposed thrust tore at the structure and the drumming of the flaring rockets mounted as he reversed the ship and altered their relative speed. Again they drove towards the enemy vessel and again the throb of guns vibrated through the ship as Carlos blasted at squat hulls with steel and flame.

'Like geese,' yelled the gunner. 'Like sitting ducks. They must be mad to try and run a blockade with converted cargo ships.'

'Don't get careless,' warned Baron

grimly. He swore and jerked at the levers as a torpedo homed towards him its rocket trail clear against the night of space. Abruptly a flower of incandescence blossomed where a ship had been a spreading gush of obliterating energy as one of the torpedoes homed on its target and detonated the fuel, ripping hull and crew, cargo and ship to unrecognisable debris.

'You must have got their radar,' said Baron with satisfaction. 'Keep it up.' He grunted as sleek shapes revealed themselves against the distant ball of the sun. 'Here comes trouble. We're up against more than just cargo ships now. Those were warships.' Tensely he concentrated on the instruments.

The rest became a nightmare. A hell of flaring rocket trails and bludgeoning acceleration changes, of whining guns and desperate escapes from the hunting torpedoes and streaming shells. Air gushed from the punctured hull and shrapnel smashed against the armoured backs of the protecting acceleration chairs. Glass shattered as the instrument panel exploded into semi-molten ruin and the radar screen died with a shower of sparks.

'Out!' Baron threw the controls into neutral and punched the crash button. Explosive charges blew out the double doors of the air lock and stars glittered coldly through the wide gap. 'Hurry, Carlos. Without radar we can't spot the torpedoes and once they home in on us it'll be curtains.'

'A moment.' The gunner's heavy breathing sounded thick and harsh over the intersuit radio. 'My leg . . . '

'Are you hurt?'

'I'm not sure, but my leg! I can't move it.'

'Let me see.' Impatiently the captain tugged at the limp form and stared at the narrow confines of the gun compartment. 'I see what's wrong. A shell must have buckled the hull and you're trapped. 'I'll get you out.' Sweat oozed from his forehead as he dragged at the trapped man. Carlos groaned, a quick inhalation and a long, pain-filled sigh, abruptly he came free as the captain dragged ruthlessly at the trapped limb.

'Madre de Dios!'

'How's the suit? Intact?'

'I think so. Yes.'

'Good. Abandon ship.' Frantically the captain swung the gunner through the blown-out opening in the hull, flinging him out and away with the full strength of his arms then, standing on the edge of the aperture, he kicked himself into the void.

Like a darting fish he glided from the ripped hull, spinning slightly as he moved, impelled by the strength of his legs and twisting as he tried to find the suited figure of the gunner. Below him Mars was a swollen orange marked by dust storms and tipped with the white of the snowcap. To one side the sun glowed like a feral eye, smaller than as seen from Earth, but brilliant in its naked glory. On all sides the stars shone, cold and remote, clear and steady in their glittering aloofness. A voice whispered from his radio.

'Baron?'

'Here, Carlos. How do you feel?'

'Rotten. I think my leg is broken, it

hurts enough for that, and there is something wrong with my spine. I can't move my other leg!'

'You'll be all right. The hospital will fix you up as good as new.'

'You think so?' Irony weighed the whispering voice. 'There is an old proverb I have heard of. First catch your rabbit.'

'Meaning that we've got to get to the hospital first?'

'Exactly.'

'Don't worry about that. The radio tracer will have reported our position and they'll be looking for us. You've got your gear? Reaction pistols and signal flares?'

'Yes, but . . . '

'We'll get together after the ship goes. I don't want to betray our position to the enemy and they won't leave until the ship has been destroyed. If we use the reaction pistols now they'll spot them and drag us in.'

'Maybe it would be better that way, my friend,' said Carlos quietly. 'Space is very big.'

'And spend the rest of the war in a prison camp?' Baron grunted. 'Not me.

I . . . ' He blinked as fire blossomed from the distant hull of the abandoned vessel. It gushed in a fury of released energy, ripping hull and plates to slumped fragments as the exploding torpedo ripped and detonated the fuel tanks. For a moment it seemed to fill all the universe then it died in expanding incandescence and the cold night of space reclaimed its own.

'Carlos?'

'Here.'

'What's the matter with you?' Baron frowned. 'You sound hurt.'

'I'm dying, my friend, you must forgive my weakness.'

'Dying!'

'Yes. A fragment from the ship. It gashed my suit and went deeper than my skin.' Incredibly the gunner laughed. 'For me it is over, all over. No longer the dreams of good wine and food, of fiesta and sloe-eyed dancing girls. Never again will I walk in the sun and feel the warm winds of summer. For me there can be only silence and . . . ' He coughed and liquid gurglings echoed with sickening suggestion from the helmet radio.

'Carlos!' Baron glared around him trying to spot the figure of the gunner. 'Use your reaction pistol, light a flare, anything, but show me where you are.'

'It would be useless, my friend. There is nothing you can do.'

'Like hell! I can patch your suit, take care of you.' Irritably the captain twisted his body, glaring at the circling stars. 'Where are you?'

'Forget it.' The whispering voice choked and strangled over rising blood. 'It is nothing, it comes to us all and each must face it alone. But — one thing'

'Yes?'

'Drink a bottle of wine for me. Go to a fiesta and learn what tortillas are, chili, tamales. Sip at tequila and listen to the guitars. Do that for me, my friend. For me.'

'Yes.' Baron gritted his teeth against the sounds of a man in pain. 'I'll do that.'

'Thank you. Do not forget.'

'Carlos.'

'Red wine,' muttered the gunner. 'Deep and rich, like blood.' He choked again, tried to laugh, and sighed in final surrender. 'Adios.'

Silence and the soft hum of the empty carrier wave.

'Carlos!'

Silence and the silent burning of the distant stars, gleaming like candles on the altars of heaven, keeping watchful vigil over one who was no more.

Bleakly Baron watched them through the transparent faceplate of his helmet, seeing them slide across his field of vision as he spun slowly on his journey through space. Stars like scattered diamonds, the ruddy ball of Mars, the tiny orb of the sun, then stars again. Over and over, a glittering panorama of majestic splendour, a blazing sea of light that had lasted untold years and would last uncounted eons more. Dully he watched them, not thinking about what he saw, not thinking about a man now dead or a promise fresh made. Just watching.

And waiting for the rescue that might never come.

2

The laboratory was a sterilised miracle of green plastic and plated steel. A place of humming electronic machines and peculiar instruments, of racked ampoules and selected cultures, of metal and glass, plastic and tissue. A modern shrine for the ill and the broken, for those who suffered and those who wanted to get well. There were always plenty of those but not all could be treated, for this was no mere hospital, this was the place where men took a faltering step towards fresh discoveries and bodies were regarded as 'interesting cases' and not as human beings.

Doctor Le Maitre walked briskly through the gleaming corridors, his step light in the Luna gravity, and the soft glow of the tube lights shining from his naked scalp. An old man, he still retained the burning enthusiasm of youth, and glittering blue eyes, glazed a little by their contact lenses, gave the lie to seamed features and wrinkled hands. He glanced at the man walking beside him, tilting his head with a peculiar bird-like motion, and his voice echoed from the spotless walls like the rustle of dry Autumn leaves.

'You're certain that the specimen is intact? No organic injury?'

'None.' Doctor Whitney smiled at the old man's eagerness. 'He is hardly a specimen though. I prefer to call him a patient.'

'Patient, specimen, what's the difference? To me they are the same. You will admit, I hope, that he is an interesting case?'

'Yes.'

'And dead?'

'Quite dead.' Whitney paused before a door. 'A ship discovered him on their radar, drifting in an orbit well beyond Mars, and had the good sense to leave him in vacuo while bringing him in. Obviously he was a member of the military forces, his papers show him to be a pilot attached to the Terran Fleet and, as far as we can judge, he must have died a few weeks prior to the armistice.' He pushed open the door. 'It was very lucky that there are no organic injuries. As a surmise I would say that he waited for rescue as long as he could and then, when his air ran out, he opened his helmet and got it over with.'

A sealed vat stood in the centre of the room. Within it, protected from the surrounding air, a man lay humped in a peculiarly huddled position, one leg drawn up a little and his hands lifted to his bare head.

'Naturally we haven't tried to alter his position in any way. Aside from searching his external pockets for information we have left him exactly as found.'

'So I see.' Le Maitre grunted with satisfaction. 'You were wise. Any attempt to adjust his limbs would have broken them off like sticks of wood. He must be as brittle as glass.' He looked at the young man, his blue eyes shining with excitement. 'This is wonderful! A complete, unharmed specimen, ready to our hand. It couldn't have worked out better.'

'You're going to try and revive him?'

'But of course, what else?'

Whitney didn't answer, but his eyes as he stared at the humped figure in the airtight case were thoughtful.

'What's the matter, my boy?' The old man stared at his assistant. 'This is a great thing for us.'

'I was thinking about him.' Whitney pointed to the dead man. 'He died five years ago now and since then has been drifting in space, frozen solid and protected from all decay and cellular breakdown. What do we know about him? His name was Baron, he was a patrol ship pilot and he fought in the Terran-Martian war. He died in space.'

He stared at the old man. 'He isn't a specimen, you know, doctor. He is a human being.'

'What of it?' The old man shrugged. 'So he is human.' He chuckled. 'If we revive him he will be grateful, if not . . . ' He spread his hands. 'What harm can we do? After all, the man is dead, legally and actually. Nothing we can do will hurt him now.'

'I'm thinking of those mice,' said

Whitney slowly. 'The guinea pigs, the cats, the monkeys and other experimental animals. We've exposed them to space and managed to revive them, but . . . '

'They were a low order of life,' snapped the old man impatiently. 'Anyway, we did manage to restore several monkeys to life and reason, the others don't count.' He smiled as he stared at the dead man. 'This is the first human we have yet found without organic injury who has obviously died before asphyxiation. His blood has not been poisoned and there is no reason to assume cellular breakdown. From all counts he is a perfect experimental subject for research and if we are able to restore him to life and reason we shall have developed a technique which will be of inestimable value in all cases of exposure to the void.'

'You don't have to convert me,' said Whitney quietly. 'I know how important it is to develop the resurrection technique, and I know just what avenues such a process will open up. Suspended animation for one, the ability to spend years, centuries even, frozen and dead, and yet awake in full possession of all faculties. It will mean that spaceships can head out towards the stars, their crews frozen but alive and able to take over on landing. It will mean lots of things and one of them will be to abolish the eternal dread of space travellers. If we succeed it won't matter what happens to a ship. All the crew and passengers need do is to expose themselves to space, die, and wait for rescue and resurrection.' A glow entered his deep-set eyes. 'In a sense it could lead to a form of immortality. A man could spread his normal life span over centuries, thousands of years, tens of thousands. He would be able to observe the rise of a galactic civilisation and watch the unfolding of discoveries we haven't even dreamed of. Brilliant scientists could be frozen until such time as new techniques had been developed to restore youth to their worn-out bodies.' He caught himself and laughed with self-conscious embarrassment. 'But first we must restore this man's life.'

'And we will!' Le Maitre almost trembled in his excitement. 'Everything is ready in the laboratory. You will arrange for the body to be stripped and made ready?'

'Yes.'

'Hurry, then. I will wait for you in the main lab.'

It took a long time before the frozen corpse of the space captain was ready. First his heavy spacesuit had to be cut away, then the anti-acceleration padding, the thick underwear and the restraining bandages. Whitney sweated as he worked, knowing that any strain would snap glass-hard tissue and cause irreparable injuries. Finally it was done, the stiff body washed with alcohol, and placed gently on supporting webbing in the immersion vat.

'We must not hurry this,' said Le Maitre as he stood by the main panel and directed operations. 'The thawing however, while not too slow must yet be quick enough to prevent tissue breakdown. Most important of all the thawing must be even, from inside out so to speak, and the temperature must be controlled at every moment.'

'Shall I put on the mask?'

'Not yet. Seal his mouth and nose against admission of the immersion fluids but it is too soon to apply the oxygen mask. That will come when he has been thawed to normal temperature.'

Whitney nodded, carefully sealing the parted lips and nostrils with the plastic filler, then glanced at the old man.

'Ready?'

'Yes.'

Relays clicked and a motor droned to sudden life. Liquid gushed from opened valves into the wide vat in which the dead man lay, covering him with a luminescent green film, thick and oily-looking. More relays thudded against their contacts, and on the wide instrument panel several needles flickered across their dials.

'High frequency current on,' murmured the old man. 'The eddy waves will penetrate every cell and thaw evenly throughout.' He glanced at the conductive fluid in the vat. 'This part is simple. All we are really doing is putting him in an electronic oven. The hard part will follow when he has thawed enough to be handled with safety.'

'The artificial lung?' Whitney glanced to where the instrument stood next to the revival vat. The old man nodded.

'Naturally. The lung, controlled heat, an artificial heart to stir the blood, electronic energen flow to restore individual cell potential, drugs to stimulate the nerves and muscles. Shock treatment to restore synapses and magnetic induction to replace lost ionic complex, and trying to restore life isn't quite the same as repairing a machine. In theory, yes, but in practice it isn't as simple as that. Unless everything is done and all cells and co-ordinate functions are restored decay and breakdown will set in and all our work be wasted.'

'And the brain?'

'Both the hardest and the easiest part. The body can be made to live after a fashion even though the brain is unaware. I am not yet certain whether the restoration of the body automatically brings with it restoration of mental awareness, or whether it may be due to some other cause. In any case, time will tell, and unless there has been disintegration of the cortex we should stand an excellent chance of success.'

He sighed and glanced at the ranked dials. Needles swung and steadied beneath the surge of current as automatic relays kept the current at optimum flow, and tiny thermometers registered the internal and external temperature of the dead man.

'Body relaxing, sir,' called a technician from beside the vat. Quickly the old man crossed to the side of the container slipping gloved hands into the luminous green fluid and touching the flesh.

'Temperature?'

'Sixty degrees.'

'Increase current.' He stood by the vat as Whitney spun rheostats. 'Temperature?'

'Sixty-five degrees.'

'Good.' Carefully the old man inserted hair-fine electrodes into the main nerves and fastened other contacts to the major sensory areas. 'Stand by with stimulants.'

Technicians, robed and masked, wheeled a flat trolley loaded with drugs and hypodermics to the side of the vat. Others adjusted the gleaming bulk of the artificial lung and all stood in tense readiness as they waited for instructions. Sweat glistened on the old man's high forehead and an assistant deftly wiped it away.

'Temperature?'

'Eighty degrees.'

'Cut current, we mustn't thaw him out too fast.' He stared at the assembled technicians. 'Blood plasma ready?'

'Yes, sir.'

'Saline and glucose?'

'Yes, sir.'

'Good.' Again the assistant wiped the high forehead free of glistening beads of perspiration. 'You know what has to be done. Once we commence the final stage of operations there can be no respite and no mistakes.' The mask over his nose and mouth moved as he licked dry lips. 'Temperature?'

'Ninety degrees.'

'Stand by with stimulants. Ready the artificial lung; ninety per cent oxygen, ten per cent helium. Prepare infra-red lamps.' He waited as the technicians moved with quiet skill about their instruments. 'Whitney?'

'Yes, Doc?'

'Operations commence when internal temperature rises to a hundred. Energen flow at two per cent. Magnetic induction at five per cent.'

'Right.' The young man set the dials. 'Are you going to change his blood?'

'Not at once. We'll inject stimulants and apply the lung first. I want to be certain that the blood isn't congealed before draining and replacing. That can be done when the artificial heart is attached.' Again the mask fluttered in a betraying gesture. 'Temperature?'

'Ninety-eight point three.'

'Attach mechanical heart.'

Rapidly the technicians made the deep incisions in the now-limp flesh and wedded the plastic tubes to the main arteries and veins.

'Remove seal and adjust lung.'

Liquid gurgled as the webbing was lifted and the sealed mouth and nose rose above the level of the luminous green fluid. Swiftly the plugging was removed from lips and nostrils, the oxygen mask strapped around the head, and the activator of the artificial lung fastened around chest and diaphragm.

'Temperature?'

'One hundred!'

Immediately the technicians swung into smooth, co-ordinated action. Skilfully hypodermics slid into veins and stimulants flooded into the bloodstream. Other drugs joined them, saline, glucose, and a potent compound to destroy the coagulating power of the blood. Le Maitre hovering over them, his burning blue eyes flickering from operation to operation, missing nothing, correlating all that had been done.

'Start the heart.'

Pumps whined and pistons moved as the compact device answered to the flow of power and emulated the normal workings of a human heart. Blood gushed into the sterilized ventricles and passed through the attached tubing as the machine forced the ruby liquid through the unresponsive flesh.

'Lung!'

Air sighed as the bellows filled and emptied. Slowly the arc of the chest lifted, fell, lifted, fell again beneath the external stimulus of the artificial lung. Gases sighed as they flowed into empty lungs, sighed again as they were expelled by the compression of the diaphragm.

'Speed?'

'Seventy-five, sir.'

'Cut to sixty-eight. No need to burn his tissues unless we have to.' Deftly the assistant wiped sweat from the old man's glistening forehead. 'Whitney.'

'Yes?'

'Energen and magnetic flow.'

'Right.'

Lights flashed on the panel of instruments as minute electrical charges began to restore the electrical potential of the dead man.

'Cut oxygen to eighty per cent. Accelerate heart. Stimulants. Begin to replace blood.' Le Maitre moved quietly about the instrument-ringed vat as he gave his terse orders. 'Skin temperature?'

'One hundred.'

'Increase to one-twenty. Internal temperature constant at one hundred.'

Green fluid seethed beneath the impact

of high frequency currents and a faint droning vibrated through the laboratory.

'Blood replaced, sir.'

'Good. Adrenaline in the heart. One CC. Nerve shock and sensory irritation.'

Whitney nodded and threw a switch. In the vat the still figure jerked and jerked again as electricity contracted muscles and flowed along nerves.

'Enough.' Le Maitre straightened and impatiently brushed aside the assistant trying to swab his forehead. 'Nothing to do now but wait until circulation and oxygeneration are complete. Reactions are promising and there are no signs of deterioration.' For the first time emotion tinged his voice with excitement. 'I think we'll do it, Whitney! I think we can restore him to life!'

'Signals from heart, sir,' called one of the technicians. 'I caught a flutter then.'

'So soon?' The old man spun back to the vat. Tensely he listened to the electric stethoscope, straining his ears to catch the amplified sound, and lifted his hand for silence. Painfully, irregularly, like the distant throb of a muffled drum, sounds came from the speaker, the halting, painfully weak flutter of a pulsing heart.

'By God!' swore one of the men. 'He's alive!'

'Not yet,' reminded Le Maitre grimly. 'This could be more reaction to stimulus, we've got to make it a self-perpetuating, involuntary muscular response to brain signals from the cortex.' He frowned. 'So much depends on the cortex,' he whispered. 'We could pump blood through this body and oxygenate it by artificial means but that is not life. No. To live he must do these things himself. If not he will be nothing but a mechanically assisted lump of flesh.'

'Heart beat steadying, sir,' whispered the technician.

'Rate?'

'As the machine.'

'Of course, it would be.' The old man listened to the metronome-like beat from the speaker. 'As soon as the beat matches that of the heart we'll cut out the lung and see whether or not his breathing is automatic.' He frowned. 'More stimulants, Whitney. Increase energen flow to six per cent. Sugar content?'

'Normal, sir.' A technician drew fresh blood from the mechanical heart. 'No signs of narcosis or organic breakdown tissue.'

'I expected none. This man didn't die, he merely — stopped. The freezing was so fast that it is doubtful whether or not any cells were ruptured in the process.'

'What about pressure, sir?' One of the technicians looked up from where he tended an infrared lamp. 'Wouldn't the removal of pressure when he lost his atmosphere have burst his organs?'

'No. Some of the skin capillaries, of course, and perhaps a few blood vessels in the nose and ears, but nothing too serious. The removal of pressure coincided with the freezing by expansion as he lost his air. In any case the human body is pretty tough and it has been proved that internal organs do not rupture with an alteration of atmospheric pressure of ten pounds. Spacesuits of the military forces use about eight instead of the normal fifteen. Less oxygen is needed while in free fall and there are psychological reasons for the reduced pressure.' Le Maitre glanced at the amplifier. 'Heart match yet?'

'Yes, sir. I've been monitoring the beat and increasing the rate to seventy-two. They are steady now.'

'Good.' The old man drew a deep breath. 'Drain vat.'

Liquid gurgled as it vanished through the escape valves and the supporting webbing tightened as it raised the lax figure level with the top of the container. An operating table slid beneath the still form and the empty vat dropped smoothly down below the floor, a panel sliding over the aperture and making the floor whole again. Tensely they gathered around the limp figure.

'Cut lung!'

The hissing pulse of the pneumotor died and the bellows hung empty and collapsed against their frame. Swiftly the technician removed the body parts of the mechanism then, eyes anxious, they watched the steady rise and fall of the chest.

Up, down. Up, down. The rib cage

reflecting the brilliant light as it moved by semivoluntary muscular action, sucking essential gases into the lungs to oxygenate the circulating blood.

'He's living,' whispered a man. 'He's breathing all on his own.'

Le Maitre shook his head with impatient irritation. 'He's breathing without artificial aid,' he corrected, 'but that's all and it means nothing. It could be reflex action continuing from pre-example. The heart is still under mechanical assistance, remember, and that in itself would stimulate the respiratory nerves.' He glanced at Whitney where he stood by the bank of electronic controls. 'Increase energen flow to ten per cent. Cut magnetic induction. Stand by for neuron stimulus.'

'Right.'

The old man frowned as the even rise and fall of the chest faltered.

'Increase oxygen. Stand by with stimulants. Accelerate heartbeat to eighty.'

Again the even breathing faltered, the rib cage glistened as it jerked and shuddered. Le Maitre grunted as he stooped over the body.

'As I suspected. The cortex is still unaware, the neuron paths 'dead'. All this muscular activity is no different from that of a frog's leg kicking when subjected to electric current. A mere parody of life instead of life itself.' He glanced towards the young doctor. 'Neural stimulus.'

Whitney nodded and adjusted his controls. On the dials before him needles kicked and steadied as they registered the minute amounts of electric energy flooding into the convolutions of the brain. Too much would sear and destroy the delicate electrical potential, short-circuiting the synapses and burning out neuron paths. Too little would be a waste of time.

Carefully he adjusted the rheostats, compensating for loss through resistance and stabbing at the motor areas with shocking current conveyed by hair-fine electrodes embedded in the brain of the limp figure.

On the table the body jerked, jerked again, and the chest rose and fell in a great sigh. Again the lungs filled, hesitated, and expelled the trapped gases in a long exhalation. Again, then the rhythm steadied, and the rib cage resumed its regular motion.

'Good.' Le Maitre chuckled behind his mask. 'This is what we need. Direct control from the brain centres instead of external stimulus.' He glanced towards the artificial heart. 'Rate?'

'Eighty, sir.'

'Strength?'

'Optimum.'

'Good. Cut heart!'

Power died in the compact machine, the blood still surging through the transparent ventricles, but now that blood was pumped not by a machine of glass and metal but one of muscle and sinew. For a long moment they stared at it in silence, ears strained to the metronome-beat from the amplifier then . . .

'He's living!' A technician almost shouted the words. 'Heart and lungs operating by normal control! We've done it! By God, we've raised a man from the dead!'

'Remove heart,' said Le Maitre calmly, but though his voice was even his hands trembled a little and his bright blue eyes glistened with triumph. Tensely he watched as the pump was removed and the plastic tubes attached to the main arteries and veins joined and sealed. Still the organic pump beat with strong regularity and he relaxed a little, his mask stirring to a shielded smile.

'Well?' Whitney stared from across the room. 'Have we succeeded?'

'Perhaps.' The scientist in the old man quashing unjustified enthusiasm. 'We have restored his body and revived heart and lung action, circulation and normal control of the prime functions, but . . . '

'The rest?'

'Yes. We still don't know whether or not his brain will function as it should. What we see now is mere animal response, a man hopelessly lost in insanity would show as much, and what good is a functioning body without a functioning brain?' He sighed. 'When I remember those guinea pigs . . . ' His voice trailed into a sick silence.

'The monkeys came through all right,' reminded the young man. 'Why not Baron?'

'Monkeys do little but eat and sleep, play and scratch. We restored those abilities, but will they be enough? This man is human, he must regain awareness, full awareness, for if he does not we have failed. Will he remember what happened to him? Will he retain the powers of speech? Of reason? Of moral right and wrong?' The old man shrugged. 'Only time will tell — and we haven't too much time.'

'Why not?'

'The brain cells are stubborn. They are the last to deteriorate but once they do nothing can restore them. The brain cannot heal itself, it cannot grow fresh tissue. Now that he has been thawed and apparent life returned we must force the brain into some kind of activation. I . . .' He broke off as he stared at the silent figure on the operating table.

Baron had opened his eyes.

3

Like empty pools of grey nothingness they were, dead and lifeless, devoid of all feeling and recognition. Like chips of volcanic glass, glistening in the reflected light of the fluorescents the pupils contracted to pinpoints, the ball a peculiar hard white tinged with blue. Sleep-walker's eyes, fish eyes, dead man's eyes, the eyes of the insane.

Two long strides Le Maitre took and his hands were gentle as they touched the muscles around the staring orbs. Impatiently he gestured towards the young man and Whitney joined him, signaling for a technician to take his place at the control panel.

'Is he awake?' He whispered as though afraid of causing that which he had hoped had taken place. The old man shook his head.

'No. There is no awareness, the lids opened by muscular reaction but the brain isn't receiving visual images.' He passed his hand over the staring eyes. 'See? No response, not even of the iris, and that colouration . . . ' He frowned.

'Glaucoma?'

'It could be, but I doubt it. Internal pressure of the anterior when the aqueous froze and expanded would give the symptoms of glaucoma but the thawing would have relieved the pressure.' He reached for an ophthalmoscope and examined the staring eyes. 'No, no sign of glaucoma or any other organic disease.' He sighed. 'This is the hard part, Whitney.'

'Yes?'

'You know damn' well it is.' The old man gestured towards the wide-eyed figure. 'Look at him. Behind those eyes lies a brain, one of the most complex electro-mechanisms ever built by man or nature. It holds everything that makes a man the thing he is. His memories, experiences, knowledge. With it he is able to co-ordinate his body, use the marvellous tools of his hands, learn and reason, guess and discover. It makes him a man and without it he is worse than a beast.' He sighed. 'Our job is to restore awareness to that brain.'

'Shock treatment?' Whitney frowned. 'I don't like that, it can cause too much damage and that is the one thing we want to avoid.'

'I agree. We dare not shock the brain any more than necessary. Baron has already experienced the greatest shock a man can undergo. He died. To everyone else that shock is the final one, there can be no greater. It is our job to convince the brain that it didn't die at all.'

'I see what you mean.' Whitney nodded. 'But is it as simple as that?'

'Of course it isn't, nothing is simple and the human brain by its mere construction can never be, but we must do what we can.' Le Maitre glanced at the huge dial of a wall chronometer. 'We must hurry. Every moment wasted means that the electro-potential is dissipating from the neuron paths and when it has gone degeneration will set in.' Abruptly he swung into action. 'Stimulus, eddy currents and directed energen flow.

Ignore the body now, it can take care of itself, but we must restore awareness to the mind.'

Tensely they set to work.

Electrodes, delicate silver wires with needle points and insulated shafts, were sunk into the skull, probing as they penetrated the brain cells and coming to rest in the major areas of perception and memory. Current flowed along them, microvolts of magnetic force, and the external electrodes of an electro-encephalogram were taped to the temples and base of the skull. A pattern writhed on a screen, the picked up and amplified emissions of the brain currents converted to impulses which directed the tiny spot of an electron beam onto a cathode. The result was a mesh of lines with jagged peaks and valleys.

'There's the alpha wave.' Le Maitre pointed towards the screen. 'Weak, too weak, and there is hardly any trace of the beta and gamma waves at all.' He stared sombrely at the writhing lines. 'Carry on, Whitney, you know what to do.'

The young man nodded and stooped over the limp figure. Carefully he adjusted the power flow through the hair-fine electrodes, varying the potential between different areas of the brain, and as he worked the writhing mass of lines on the electro-encephalogram jumped and wavered on the screen. Time passed as he manipulated the electrodes, the current flow, the magnetic fields and energen trickle-charge he had concentrated on the base of the skull. Relentlessly the sweep hand of the wall-chronometer swung round as it counted off the minutes, the hours, and still the inert body showed no signs of returning awareness. Le Maitre sagged as he stared at the clock.

'The time,' he whispered. 'Almost it will be too late.'

'We're getting nowhere.' Whitney straightened and glanced at the old man. 'We could play like this for hours until the cell tissue deteriorated and all hope was gone. I want permission to try drastic measures.'

'Such as?'

'Neuron surgery.' He spoke quickly before the old doctor could protest. 'It's our only chance now. Somehow, somewhere, a mental block has been thrown up between the conscious and subconscious minds. We've got to break it down, and we daren't wait too long before doing it. Unless we can bring physical awareness back to the cortex all our work will have been for nothing. Baron will spend the rest of his life as a mindless idiot, a working lump of flesh, without vision, hearing, sensory perception or any of the five senses. He would be better dead. In effect he would be dead — if you can imagine a dead man with a beating heart and breathing lungs.'

Slowly Le Maitre nodded, his blue eyes pained as they stared above his mask, and Whitney could guess at the old man's feelings. Neuron surgery was a highly specialised form of therapy, needing delicate instruments and fantastic skill.

Few men were capable of it and if it proved essential in the restoration of life to all who suffered death in space, then the dream of suspended animation was ended before it begun.

'This is an emergency,' said Whitney rapidly as he assembled his instruments. 'Normally we wouldn't have to contend with the mind-shock obviously present here. The barrier must be directly due to the fact that the brain has accepted the fact that it is dead and refuses to believe otherwise. Once we restore this man he will be able to tell us of his experiences and we can avoid any repetition later on. A simple drug would prevent it, a bromide or one of the nerve hypnotics, anything to bring unconsciousness before actual death.'

He swung a screen of milk-white substance over the cranium and snapped a switch. Immediately the surface glowed with a greenish fluorescence and Whitney nodded as he adjusted the vernier controls.

'We'll set the scanning beam for brain surface and deepen the penetration if necessary. I'm still afraid of causing damage for fine as these electrodes are, yet they still ruin some of the cells.' Carefully he adjusted a control and on the screen the image writhed and blurred, lost shape and form, to steady in abrupt, razor-sharp focus at the touch of a second control.

Silently they stared at the magnified image of a naked human brain. It pulsed gently as they looked at it, bathed by an invisible flood of energy which, penetrating the bone of the skull, transmitted the image of the hidden organ back onto the fluorescent screen. In itself the instrument was nothing, merely an adaptation of the old-fashioned X-ray, but it avoided trepanning, guesswork, and blind searching for suspected faults of the internal organs. In neuron surgery it was an essential tool. Essential too were the calibrated electrodes, clamped to the skull and operated by remote control. Delicate, hair-fine things, capable of transmitting stimulating energy, cauterising infected brain cells, even severing large portions of the tissue from the main body. So fine were they that it was possible to destroy a single cell deep within the brain, and to learn the skill of their operation was something few men could do.

Whitney was one of them.

Tensely he slid his fingers in the robot gloves and, as was his habit, kept up a continual monologue as he worked. In itself it was nothing, a device for easing the terrible nerve-strain accompanying the delicate operation, but Le Maitre was glad of it and he watched and listened with eager eyes and ears.

'The brain is a funny thing,' he murmured, more to himself than to his listeners. 'It can't feel pain, there are no sensory nerves in it, and yet it receives messages from every part of the body which, in case of damage or injury, it translates as pain. Unlike the rest of the body it can't repair itself and once damaged stays that way. Most of it serves no apparently useful purpose, we can remove a major portion and the patient experiences no ill effect. Of the entire mass we use only about a tenth, most of it concentrated in the occiptital lobes.'

He grunted as a tiny dial flashed red and his muscles flexed as he fed current to one of the electrodes.

'Must build up the potential of that area. There!' He relaxed and continued his minute search of the convoluted surface. 'In effect the brain is an electronic computer. It receives and stores sensory impressions, millions of them, and it never forgets anything either seen or felt or heard. Never. The records are kept from the moment of awareness, before birth even, until the moment of death. With patience and training every single episode ever experienced during life can be recalled in full sound, taste, colour, feel, and emotion. Memory is merely the taking of selected impressions from the mental storehouse.'

An assistant wiped globules of perspiration from his streaming forehead and the image altered as he deepened the scanning depths of the rays.

'An electronic computer,' he murmured. 'It can be overloaded, blow a fuse, get fouled up by false signals and have parts of it cut off from the main circuit. It can even get unplugged from the body itself. Our job is to plug it back in.'

Again the image writhed and again the watching assistant wiped sweat from the young man's forehead. Now the screen showed the deeper parts of the brain structure, and the calibrated electrodes moved a little beneath the guidance of the young doctor's flexing muscles.

'Potential at correct variance,' he continued. 'Nothing wrong there. A little scar tissue from ruptured blood cells, probably caused by high acceleration and course-change. No signs of self-induced injury, alcohol or drugs taken in excess, and no trace of radiation burns.' He sighed. 'In other words the damn' thing should work as good as new — but it doesn't.'

He relaxed from the controls, breathing deeply from the nerve-rasping concentration, and hardly seemed to be aware of the old man's rapt attention.

'What can we do now, Whitney?'

'Do?' The young man blinked and stared at the worried eyes of the old man. 'I don't know, unless . . . ' He let his voice fade into silence as he stared at the glowing screen. 'There might be just one way, unpredictable, but worth trying. If I burned out the censor it might be just possible that the mental barrier between what the conscious imagines to be the truth and what the subconscious now knows is false, can be eliminated.'

'Burn out the censor?' Le Maitre shook his head. 'I don't like it.'

'Neither do I,' admitted the young doctor, 'but I can see no help for it. This isn't a normal case of traumatic shock. The conscious mind has accepted the reality of death and it refuses to respond to external stimuli. The subconscious, because of its innate functions with the involuntary muscles, knows that the body is not dead, but the censor is preventing that knowledge from passing to the conscious. There is conflict, a feed-back surge of opposed potential, and the result . . . ' He gestured towards the limp figure.

'But . . . ' The old man swallowed. 'Will it cause permanent damage?'

'Physically, no. Mentally it should not harm him either, but there has been no previous case of a censor removed and we can only surmise what may happen. He will have to guard against impulse, of course, force himself to weigh his every action for with the censor gone there will be no 'safety fuse' between emotion and action. That isn't too important, we can replace it with post hypnotic suggestion and induced depressants.' He looked at the old man. 'Well?'

Le Maitre glanced at the clock, then at the silent technicians, and finally, the limp figure of the somnolent man. 'You have my permission,' he said tiredly, and leaned closer as the young doctor slid his hands into the robot gloves.

'A fascinating study, the human mind,' he murmured, and the image on the screen writhed to a deeper penetration. 'As far as we can determine the portion of the brain containing the censor, the bridge between the subconscious and conscious portions of the brain, is here.' He narrowed his eyes as he adjusted the depth of the calibrated electrodes. 'Just below and to the rear of the pineal gland. We don't know yet just what it is and how it operates, but it is the barrier between desire and fulfilment. The censor is the thing that prevents a man from committing murder at a whim, stealing at a thought, insulting his fellows without apparent cause. It is the barrier between primitive emotional drive and civilised restraint. Now.'

Sweat oozed from his forehead as he guided the thin electrodes towards the indicated section of the brain. Relays thudded and needles swung on their dials as current surged through the insulated leads, cauterising the brain cells holding the mysterious function that men knew only as the 'censor'. Whitney relaxed and stared thoughtfully at the screen.

'I've burned out that portion of the brain and in effect cut the frontal lobes off from the rear portions. That means the entire rear portion of the brain is now out of all contact with the occipital lobes. I wonder . . . '

'It won't harm him,' said Le Maitre, and glanced again at the chronometer. 'Let's try to revive him.'

'A moment.' Whitney flexed his hands and slid them again into the robot gloves. 'I'm going to trace a path to replace the connecting area of the censor.'

'By-pass it, you mean?'

'Yes. I can stimulate the cells with varying potential and open a neuron channel to the subconscious. The adjusted potential will open fresh paths for the neuron synapses and replace the cauterised censor. It won't act the same, of course, but it will give access to the 'dead' areas.' The cold light of the scientist burned in his deep-set, brown eyes, and he stared at the limp figure on the operating table as if it were merely an intricate piece of mechanism instead of a human being. 'I'm going to do it! The results shouldn't harm him and they may prove very — interesting.' Grimly he bent to his work.

It took four hours. It took ten years of mental life with tension mounting like a living thing in the sterilized perfection of the operating theatre. It took the accumulated skill of mind and hand, eye and brain, the combination of human achievement and electronic perfection. When it was over weariness closed over the doctors and even the technicians seemed to have wilted beneath the strain.

'Finished.' Whitney slumped back as an assistant bathed his forehead with alcohol and refreshing agents, breathed deeply at a puff of revivifying gas, and gestured towards the assembled equipment. 'Clear away.'

'What now?' Le Maitre checked the respiration and heartbeat. 'No change.'

'We're going to wake him up,' said the young man. 'Shock electrodes on all main nerve endings. Stimulants, as much as he can stand. Flare-lamp for visual attention. Amplifiers to aural nerves. Move!'

Swiftly the technicians moved about the quietly breathing patient, adjusting and fitting the various mechanisms to the warm flesh.

'Ready, sir.'

'Good.' Whitney sighed and squeezed his eyes tightly shut. 'Let's get on with it.' Tensely he stooped over the body and whispered into the microphone, his words caught and amplified, transmitted directly to the nerves in the ears and so to the brain, jarring it with repeated sound.

'Baron! Wake up!'

Light flared from the curious lamp swung above the staring eyes. A carefully judged vibration of calculated angstrom units designed to stimulate the optic nerve without damage. Current stabbed at nerve and muscle, sheer pain to jar the sleeping ego locked in the sleeping brain.

'Baron! Wake up!'

Pain and light, stimulus and harsh command, stabbing and calling in a desperate effort to wake up a man who believed he was dead and refused to admit otherwise.

'Baron! Wake up!'

On and on, again and again, light and sound, pain and nerve-twitching current. Sweat dripped unheeded from the young doctor's forehead as he appealed directly to the ego of the once-dead man, calling to it to stir, to arouse itself from the black clouds of oblivion, to wake and regain control of its body, to see through the eyes, to hear through the ears, to feel and experience the messages from its body.

'Baron! Wake up!'

A message travelling no more than a few centimetres in distance, and yet having to travel across the immense gulf separating the living from the dead. Travelling on the wings of pain and thundering sound, searing nerve constrictions and flaring light. With every force at his command Whitney attacked the sealed fortress of the hidden brain, trying with desperate insistence to arouse the slumbering ego to awareness and a sense of personal existence.

'Baron! Wake up!'

'Heartbeat faltering, sir,' whispered a technician quietly. Whitney ignored him, repeating his message with monotonous frequency and yet taking care to vary the words so as to avoid hypnotic suggestion.

'Wake up now. Baron. Come on now. Snap out of it.'

'Sugar content falling,' whispered the technician. 'Respiration irregular.'

'Inject glucose,' ordered Le Maitre harshly. He watched with eyes reflecting his inner strain, and pushed aside the assistant with the coolants and swabs for his streaming face. 'Adrenaline. Watch saline content.'

The technician nodded and skilful hands selected loaded hypodermics.

'Wake up!' snarled Whitney harshly. 'Baron!'

A groan sighed through the room, echoing above the muted drone of electronic instruments and the soft movements of men. A thin, ghost sound, whispering as if from a vast distance and seeming to hold a terrible weariness and desire for sleep.

'Eyes closed, sir,' said a technician excitedly. He adjusted a switch on the flarelamp and the wash of light changed a little as the beam-depth adjusted to strike beneath the closed lids, the light rippling in an irregular pattern.

'Spray his throat,' snapped Le Maitre curtly. 'Blood heat saline.'

Again the groan echoed through the room and on the smooth surface of the operating table the body twitched, the head rolling a little against the restraining pads, and like the slowly closing claw of some alien insect, the fingers of the right hand clenched a little in mute protest at rest disturbed.

'He's coming out of it!' Whitney wiped the back of a gloved hand across his streaming forehead. 'Stand by with anti-shock therapy. Watch that temperature and blood density.' He clutched the microphone. 'Wake up, Baron! Wake up, damn you! Quit malingering!'

The eyes opened again, empty and dull then, as slowly as the disintegration of suns, life returned. It came like a thin fog, a subtle alteration as if a new tenant peered from behind the dusty curtains of a neglected house. Blankness crept away and intelligence came into its own again.

'Car . . .' The lips gaped and the throat worked with painful intensity. 'Carl . . .'

'Wake up, damn you!' Whitney snarled with simulated anger as he called into the microphone, adding the lash of his own voice to the whips of the electronic stimuli. 'Snap out of it!'

Lip writhed back from teeth in snarling, animal-like rage. The hands clenched and fire smouldered in the cold, slate-grey eyes. On the cheek the scar twisted like a livid signal of warning and the sound of breathing was a rasping curse.

'Who are you?' Whitney sweated as he rapped the question. Above all it was essential that the man should have awareness of his own identity. The thing on the operating table, writhing and twitching in newly awakened awareness could be no more than an animal, a brainless beast responding to the surge of primeval emotion. He snarled as he repeated the question. 'Your name, damn you! What is your name?'

'Bar . . . '

'What?'

'Ba . . . ' Warm saline bathed the vocal cords and gentle fingers massaged the constricted throat.

'Who?'

'Baron. Baron. Baron.' It sounded like the distorted playing of some ancient record. Whitney sagged, gesturing for the electronic stimulus to be cut, and swung aside the flare-lamp. Almost it was over but — he had to make certain that there was no relapse.

'Who are you?'

'Baron.'

'What is your name?'

'Baron.' Rage glowed in the grey eyes. 'Leave me alone.'

'Who are you?'

'Baron, damn you. Baron! Now leave me alone!' He sagged, the lids falling over the anger-filled eyes, and a ripple coursed through his body as relaxation came and with it a healing sleep. Whitney stared down at him, the microphone swinging forgotten from his gloved hands. Le Maitre touched him on the shoulder.

'Yes?'

'Yes. Usual post-operative treatment. Intravenous feeding, we must replace his wasted tissues, there must have been some dehydration while in space.' Sombrely he watched as expert hands stripped the equipment and instruments from the unconscious man. He felt tired, almost too tired to think straight, and before him the features of the old man seemed to waver and blur. Tiredly he closed his eyes, conscious of only one thought.

The man would live.

4

The resurrected man lay on a narrow bed in the cool greenness of the Luna Laboratory and stared at a ceiling which had the colour of a delicate leaf seen at early dawn. He wore a civilian blouse and trousers, green as the walls were green, made of shimmering synthosilk and fitting his wide shoulders and narrow waist with trim perfection. A belt circled his waist, soft shoes hugged his feet, a glinting chronometer was strapped to his left wrist. He was shaved, his hair cropped, his body filled out with good food and regulated exercise. Books rested on a low table at the side of the cot, and the blank surface of a television screen occupied a large section of one wall. He was as comfortable as a man could be, and yet he was unhappy.

He stared at the tinted ceiling and within his skull thoughts darted like summer lightning, stabbing from the sullen clouds of memory and weaving strange and convoluted patterns of mental imagery. He sat up as the door slid open and Whitney entered the room. Le Maitre followed the young man, and Baron thinned his lips at their clinical expressions.

'What do you want?' He said it harshly, not troubling to hide his impatience and irritation. Le Maitre glanced significantly at the young man, and both doctors seated themselves at a small table.

'Just dropped in to see if you are all right,' said Whitney calmly. 'How do you feel?'

'Fed up.'

'Physically I mean.'

'Well enough.' Baron flexed the muscles of his arms. 'When do I get out of here?'

'Do you want to go?' Le Maitre leaned forward as he stared at the big man. 'Aren't you comfortable here? If there is anything you would like just let us know.'

'Trying to bribe me?' Baron lowered his thick brows as he glared at the old man. 'Or are you forgetting that there's a war on and I'm needed in the Terran Fleet?'

'The war was over five years ago,' said Whitney quietly. 'The Martian colonists renounced their independence, and resumed trade with Earth.' He gestured the old man to silence. 'We haven't bothered you up to now because it was important that you recover your full physical health. Now you are as fit as we can make you.'

'So?'

'So I'd like you to help us.'

'How?'

'By permitting us to examine your mind.' He saw the captain's expression and hurried on before he could interrupt. 'You are a unique case. In fact you are the only case medical science has knowledge of.' He hesitated. 'You were dead for five years and are alive again. We want to know just what has happened to you because of that.'

To his surprise Baron didn't appear shocked at the revelation. He sat, stiff and unyielding, on the edge of the bed, and the soft light glinted from his cold grey eyes. For a long moment the silence lasted, each waiting for the other to speak, and Le Maitre swallowed as he broke it.

'Aren't you surprised?'

'No.'

'You remember then,' said Whitney eagerly. 'You recall just what happened up until the moment when you lost consciousness?'

'Yes.'

'Good. We were afraid — ' He smiled. 'You will help us then?'

'Why should I?' Baron stared coldly at the two men. 'When can I leave?'

'Soon.' The young man stared curiously at the captain. 'I can understand your impatience, but not your antagonism. Why are you so against the idea of answering a few questions and submitting to a few tests? They can't hurt you and they could help us so much. Help us and others who may need our skill and knowledge.' He smiled. 'Are you afraid?'

'Afraid?' Baron creased his lips in a humourless smile. 'Of what?'

'Of memory, perhaps?' Whitney let the words hang on the air while he stared at the scarred face of the big man. 'You underwent a terrible shock; as a doctor I know that even better than you can realise. Your libido was severely traumatised and I can understand your reticence in avoiding a repetition of that shock. But I can assure you that reliving the episode is the quickest and best way of getting rid of it — permanently.'

'Is that a good thing?' Baron shrugged. 'I'm not afraid of memories.'

'No? Then why the antagonism at telling us what occurred?'

'My memories are my own, not yours.' Abruptly the big captain rose to his feet and began to pace the room. 'Why are you so insistent on this? How will knowing what I felt at the moment of death help you? Is it just idle curiosity, or — '

'Not that.' Whitney interrupted with calculated timing. 'You are an intelligent man, Baron, and you must know that the mind cannot be divorced from the body. It isn't enough just to heal a wound, we must also heal the mental scars attendant on it. More now than ever before we realise that the mind is dominant over the body. Psychosomatic science has taught us that unless the mind is well the body can never be. Physically you seem fit, but how long will that last? At any moment you may begin to suffer from asthma, glaucoma, bronchitis, ulcers, migraine. All caused by the apparently forgotten mental experiences you underwent at the moment of death. Don't try to forget what happened, Baron. Remember, and help both yourself and us.'

'I see.' The captain paused and something like pain dragged at the corners of his thin mouth. 'What do you want me to do?'

'Relax,' said Le Maitre eagerly. 'Just let yourself forget the present and relive what you experienced five years ago. Talk about it, tell us what you felt and what you thought.'

He glanced at Whitney. 'Is there time for full recall?'

'No, and it isn't necessary. It would take too long and besides, he hasn't forgotten the episode, he just has a natural disinclination to remember it.' He glanced towards the big man. 'Ready?'

'What do you want me to do?'

'Just talk.' Whitney threw the switch on a portable recorder. 'Start at the time when you were drifting in space.'

'After Carlos died?' Baron slumped down on the narrow bed. 'I waited for a long time, just drifting through the void and watching the stars spin past my face plate. It's lonely out there, too lonely, and I'd just heard the only friend I ever had die in isolated misery. It did something to me.' He touched the region of his heart. 'I seemed to be cold and indifferent, I just didn't care any more. I just seemed to be frozen, lifeless, drained of energy.' He stared at his hands.

'Ten years,' he whispered. 'I never thought I'd miss him so much.'

'And then?'

'After about twenty hours the air began running out. I lit what flares I had and even tried to use the reaction pistol to throw me back towards Mars. Useless, of course, they were too weak to even begin cutting my velocity. I think I knew then that I was going to die.'

'How did you accept the fact,' whispered Le Maitre. 'Did you — '

'I didn't scream or rave or pray if that's what you mean.' Baron stared his contempt. 'I'd faced death too often to be afraid of it when it came. No. I was annoyed more than anything else. There was something I'd promised to do and I was furious because now it looked as if I'd never get round to doing it. Anyway, the whole thing was a mess. I suppose you could say I felt anger more than anything else.'

'No fear?' Whitney asked the question as though he were asking about the weather. 'No panic? Just anger, is that right?'

'Yes.'

'Then what?'

'I hung on for a while; hope is a funny thing and I still thought that I might be picked up. I wasn't, of course, and when the air really did run out I couldn't stand it any longer.' He swallowed, and great beads of perspiration shone on his scarred face. 'It's not nice when the air runs out. You get sick in the lungs, start retching, and you can taste your own blood. I decided to end it all quick and clean.' He paused. 'I opened my helmet and breathed space.'

'What were you thinking of then?'

'When I opened the helmet?' Baron shrugged. 'Nothing, I guess, but I seem to remember that I had the crazy idea that I could breathe once I'd done it. I didn't stop to think about it, I was pretty bad, and it happened almost of itself. I just jerked the face plate open and then — '

'Yes?' Whitney breathed the single word and the recorder made a soft purring.

'I felt the air rush past me, felt it leave my lungs, and for one moment I actually breathed space. It was a peculiar feeling, so quiet, no cold at all, just silence and a great stillness. It lasted for perhaps a second, I don't know, but during that time I felt free and clean and filled with a great sense of wonder It was awe, worship, peace; I don't know what it was, and then — ' He snapped his fingers. 'I woke up with you calling my name.'

'Nothing else?' Le Maitre sounded disappointed. 'Nothing between the time you opened your face plate until you awoke on the table?'

'No.'

'Are you certain? Please try to remember.'

'I've told you.' Baron stared at the old man. 'Sorry, but I can't bolster your superstitions. No Heaven and no Hell. Nothing.'

'But then, of course, you weren't really dead,' said the old doctor. 'The brain cells were intact and the web of electro potential had not dissipated.' He sounded a little forlorn, as a man might sound who clutched at straws to bolster his hopes. Baron laughed, Whitney did not.

'I'm sorry, Doc,' he said gently, 'but Baron was dead. Heartbeat, respiration, reaction, all had stopped. Medically and legally he was dead. You can't escape from that fact.'

'But not truly dead; if he had been we would never have been able to revive him.'

'You know better than that,' said Whitney quietly. 'As a doctor you know that we have resurrected a man and, as a doctor, I can't argue the problematical existence of a soul. We must leave that to the theologians, who, I have no doubt, will use your own arguments to prove that we have proved nothing.' He shrugged. 'Our concern must be with the living.' He stared at Baron. 'Is there anything else you would like to add?'

'No.'

'I see.' He switched off the recorder. 'Well, that will be all for now. We'll have another session tomorrow.'

'Will we?' The big man's voice held a taut bleakness. 'When do I get out of here?'

'Must we go over all that again?' Whitney sighed and forced himself to remain calm. 'Like it or not you owe a duty to science. As an officer you should know that meaning of duty. Please let us have no more of this.'

It was a mistake; he knew it as soon as he felt the words leave his lips, but he was tired, irritable, and neglected to remember that Baron was not a laboratory specimen but a living human being. He tried to cover up.

'You agreed to help us, you know. I assume that you still want to aid science and others who might benefit from what you can tell us.'

'You think wrong.' Baron surged to his feet and his thick finger trembled as he pointed at the recorder. 'Who the hell do you think you are? God? And what am I supposed to be, an animal? Damn you for your insolence. Am I a guinea pig to be kept here against my will? You've cured me and I want to get out of here. Are you going to stop me?'

'I should think that at least you would feel grateful for what we've done,' said Le Maitre with simple dignity. 'After all, we did save your life.'

'Did you?' Broken glass gritted in the savage tones. 'Did I ask you to?'

'Well, no, but — '

'Then why should I feel gratitude? I didn't ask you to resurrect me. I didn't come begging you to help me. What you did was because you wanted to do it. You wanted it, not I. Why then should I be grateful?'

Logically his argument was correct.

Whitney knew it and yet he felt the burning of irritated rage as he stared at the big man. In all fairness he strove to remember that Baron couldn't help acting the way he did, and, staring at him, the young doctor remembered the bypassed censor and the experimental operation he had performed. He swallowed his anger.

'You were dead,' he reminded. 'We brought you back to life again. Is that nothing?'

'It's too much.' Anger glowed in the cold grey eyes. 'I was dead you say, well what of it. I died, didn't I? You didn't kill me, you didn't owe me anything so why did you have to interfere? I was dead and it was over with. Now?' He gulped and sweat shone on his scarred cheeks. 'Now it's all to do again. Should I thank you for that? Must I get down on my knees and grovel because you've permitted me to experience death twice? Is that something to be grateful for?' He clenched his big hands and stared at his interlaced fingers. 'It was over,' he whispered. 'Finished. Now it has to be faced again.' He glared at the two men. 'Damn you! Damn you to hell! Don't you realise what you've done?'

'Calm yourself.' Whitney's curt tones slashed through the air like a knife. 'No hysterics, we are not children or neurotic women, and we can remain sensible.' He looked at Le Maitre. 'Perhaps we had better go now?'

'Yes,' whispered the old man, and rose to his feet. 'Perhaps we had.'

'What about me?' Baron stood before the door, the thin material of his blouse tight over his tensed muscles and his eyes were hard as he stared at the two men. 'When do I get out of here?'

'Are you certain that you want to go?' Whitney tried to find the psychological key that would convince the big man he should stay. 'Even now you're not really fit. A few more weeks — '

'No.'

'We could keep you here,' whispered Le Maitre. Baron sneered his contempt and primeval emotions made his face a distorted mask.

'Could you?' he said softly, and his big hands curved into claws. Whitney shook his head.

'Have no fear of that. This isn't a prison and you are free to go.' He felt forgotten emotions prickle his spine. 'It will take a little time, you need papers, clothes, passage to Earth. A day or so, no longer.' He hesitated. 'One other thing. I want you to keep in touch with me. Any hospital on Earth will provide a communication channel should you wish to contact me at any time, but I would appreciate it if you would let me hear from you at least once a month.' He made himself smile. 'Will you do that?'

'Perhaps.' Some of the rage left the slate-grey eyes and the scar puckered on the check. 'Sorry. I'll keep in touch I promise.'

'Thank you.' The young man hesitated. 'One other thing.'

'Yes?'

'Try and control yourself, your emotions, I mean. Don't let yourself get angry or upset. Will you promise me that too?'

'Sure, if you will do something for me.'
'If I can.'

'Where can I buy some wine, Chianti I think it's called, and some other stuff.'

Baron frowned. 'Tor — Tort — '

'Tortillas?' Whitney smiled. 'That's Mexican food and Italian wine. You'll be able to get them in any Latin American quarter. Why?'

'Nothing,' said the big man. 'No reason at all.' He was frowning as they left the green-tinted room with a ceiling like a fresh young leaf in the early light of dawn.

He was still frowning when the lights went out.

5

A rocket took him to Earth, one of the stubby, short-shot vessels plying between Luna and the mother planet. A thin-hulled ship with small tanks and big cargo space, conveying the assembled produce of the planets from the inspection depot of Tycho down to New London, Greater New York, or the wide landing field in the desert wastes of Arizona. Other landing fields dotted the Earth, Woomera in Australia, Glynod, in Poland, or what used to be Poland. Kung Sing in China, and the big, dusty one in Africa. From them the short-shot rockets blasted towards the Moon, boosters falling away when they reached optimum velocity, and from Tycho the interplanetary liners took over.

Baron was headed for Greater New York.

He sat, half asleep in the bucket seat, not thrilling as the other half-dozen passengers thrilled to the sough and whine of braking atmosphere as they swung in for landing. He had experienced it all before, ten years of it during the drawn-out Terran-Martian war, and he was hardened to the throb and drum of rockets. The landing was not a particularly good one, the pilot slamming them down too hard for comfort, and the big man glowered at him with professional distaste.

Impatiently he joined the line waiting to be cleared by the port authorities, showing his identification papers and matching his thumbprint with that on the plastic.

'Baron?' The official grunted as he stamped the identity card. 'Want to duck out the back way?'

'Why should I?'

'You're the resurrected man, aren't you?'

'Am I?' The big man slipped the papers in his pocket. 'Is that what they call me?'

'Yeah.' The official jerked his thumb towards the entrance. 'There's a reception committee waiting out there for you. If you want to act shy there's a back way out.'

'I'm not timid.' The big man swung towards the door. 'Thanks all the same.'

'You're welcome.' The official shrugged as he turned to the next in line, forgetting the big man, the crowds, the girl he had to meet after duty hours, everything in the monotonous rush and routine of business.

Baron stepped outside.

A crowd surged towards him, a pushing, shoving crowd of shrill-voiced women and impatient men. Flash bulbs bloomed in his face like dying stars, and a babble of questions rose around him like the frenzied mouthings of idiots at prayer.

'What's it like to be alive?'

'Did you see St. Peter?'

'Any message for the faithful?'

'Do you use Mirico-shave?'

'Just smile, please.'

A woman thrust her way towards him, some small-time video actress after free publicity. Her painted face was twisted in an artificial smile, schooled to show too-white teeth and too-red lips. Perfume wafted from her, heavy and reeking, and the synthosilk on her body did nothing to hide her figure. Baron grunted as she threw her arms around him.

'What the hell?'

'Take it easy, big boy,' she whispered. 'Hold the pose.'

'Go to hell!' He shoved her aside, thrust his way through the crowd and flagged a passing turbo-cab.

'Where to, bud?'

'Fleet Headquarters. Hurry.'

In the calm of the vehicle he relaxed. The crowd had surprised him; somehow the news of his resurrection and arrival must have leaked from the Luna Laboratories and excited the interest of the mob. He was news, big news, and the thought of it left a taste in his mouth. He was glad when the turbo-cab skidded to a halt outside the towering building that was Terran Headquarters.

A receptionist listened to him with bored inattention.

'Captain Baron. Yes, we've heard of you, but the time — ' She glanced towards a wall chronometer. 'I suggest you come back tomorrow.'

'I suggest you shift your rear and do some work,' he said tightly. 'Where can I find someone with enough brass to get the wheels moving?'

'If you will make proper application through channels,' she said coldly, 'your case will be attended to.'

'It will be attended to now!' Suddenly he was behind the desk, his fingers hard as they clutched the nape of her neck. 'Play a tune on that intercom, sister, and move!'

Something in his voice, or perhaps it was the iron grip of his fingers, not hurting yet but giving harsh promise of what could be, stirred her to action. Lights glowed on the intercom and voices responded to her urgent summons as messages were relayed over the vast building. Meekly she stared up at him.

'Captain Morris will see you in room fifty-nine.' She rubbed at the back of her neck. 'Are you always so polite?'

He didn't answer, walking swiftly across the echoing hall towards room fifty-nine.

Captain Morris was an armchair officer, a fat man with a neat uniform and a pompous manner to match, and he pursed his lips as Baron strode into the office.

'I must remind you, captain,' he said primly, 'that you are not in action now. An officer is supposed to be, and act like, a gentleman.' He rested the tips of plump fingers together and examined them with meticulous care. 'I understand you wish to see me?'

'Yes.'

'Your problem?'

'I want money, information, reassignment.' Baron dropped into a chair. 'You know about me?'

'I have your dossier.' Morris condescended to look at his visitor. 'I assure you that all this haste is entirely unnecessary. The machinery which has been set up to deal with retired officers is capable of dealing with your case in the normal way.'

'Retired?'

'Naturally. The war is over, captain.' He didn't trouble to hide his sneer. 'The

Terran Fleet has been forced to reduce its personnel, and your age — ' He flipped the pages of the file. 'Well, you are rather old, aren't you?'

'I'm thirty, in good physical condition, a trained pilot and a front-rank fighter.' Baron forced himself to be calm. 'A medical examination will prove what I say.'

'Your file gives your age as thirty-five, and a medical examination will not be necessary.' Fat fingers crawled like slugs over the white papers. 'You were reported killed in action and, naturally, your name was dropped from the active list.' He smiled. 'I think that is all captain.'

'You what!'

'Officially you are dead.' Morris gestured towards the file enjoying his moment. He didn't enjoy it long. Baron moved with the swiftness of a striking snake, his cold grey eyes burning with cold fury. One hand caught the fat man by the front of the tunic, the other rested on his throat.

'You fat swine! Are you trying to be funny? You know damn well that I'm not dead.'

'Please.' Morris gulped and tried to smile. 'Naturally we know that, I only repeated what was in your file.' He gasped as the grip round his throat fell away. 'Really, Baron, I must ask you to remember who and what I am.'

'I know what you are,' said Baron coldly. 'When I think of it I feel ill. Get on with what you have to do and don't try any more jokes. I'm not in a laughing mood.'

'Right.' Anger glowed in the little eyes wreathed in their circles of fat. 'Here it is then. As a ward of the State all your possessions reverted to the State when you were declared legally dead. Your commission was rescinded at the same time. In brief, you are no longer connected with the Terran Fleet in any way, and all back pay and saved monies were restored to the Treasury.'

'You're joking.' Baron wiped his forehead and stared at his moist hand. 'How could that happen, I'm not dead.'

'Officially you are. You died in action five years ago.' Morris shrugged. 'There it is, Baron, the official fact as in your file.'

'But they know different. I was found, restored to life, fit as ever I was.' He licked his lips. 'There must be some mistake.'

'Do you deny that you died?'

'No. I can't. I know that I died, but — ' He thinned his lips as he stared at the fat officer. 'It's a trick. I'm alive and I want full back pay, accumulations and five years' service pay with extras for front-line duty.'

'Impossible!'

'Why? I would have got it had I been a prisoner of war.'

'You couldn't have been a prisoner that long. The war ended a week after you were reported dead, and anyway, how can a dead man claim service pay?'

'Don't ask me riddles.' Baron stared at the fat man and his hands tightened on the edge of the desk. 'Don't try me too far, Morris. I want a straight answer to a straight question. Do I get any money?'

'Yes.'

'That's better.' His grip relaxed and he smiled. 'How much?'

'I have been authorised to make you an

ex-gratia payment of two thousand and five hundred credits.'

'What!'

Morris removed a slip of paper from beneath a clip. 'Here it is. You can cash this draft at any bank, shop, hotel or, if you wish, it can be cashed at the desk in the hall.' He held out the printed slip.

'Two-thousand five hundred!' Baron made no attempt to take the draft. 'A month's pay! Damn it, they owed me tens of thousands and I have a long-service bonus due as well. I won't take it.'

'Suit yourself.' Morris shrugged and let the slip fall to the desk. 'If you take my advice, however, you'll take it. You know the regulations as well as I do and there isn't a hope of you getting more.' He raised his hand at the big man's gesture of protest. 'I know what you're going to say, but look at it in a logical light. You died. Immediately your estate reverted to the next of kin, which, in your case, was the State. The fact that you were found and resurrected, a thing never known before, doesn't alter that fact. You have no money due to you and this payment,' he touched the draft, 'is strictly off the record and admits of no liability on the part of the authorities whatsoever.'

'The way I look at it I'm owed about a hundred and fifty thousand credits. I want it.'

'From whom?' Morris sighed with a lawyer's impatience as he stared at the captain. 'The moment you were declared dead you lost all claim on the Terran Fleet. A dead man simply can't remain on the payroll. I've already explained about your estate, and even if you had left it to an individual you couldn't recover it. The statute of limitations, you know, and anyway, there simply isn't a precedent of a dead man returning to life after five years. I'm sorry, Baron, but there it is. If I were you I'd be glad to be alive without worrying over money.'

'Would you?'

'Certainly, and so would any man.' The fat officer picked up the draft. 'Here, don't be foolish. Take it and forget about the whole thing.'

'I'll take the case to law.'

'That's up to you, of course, but

frankly you wouldn't stand a chance, Confidentially, the Terran Fleet has been severely cut on approbations and there just isn't the money to spare.' He hesitated. 'If you'd like a suggestion?'

'Yes?'

'You are unique and have quite a bit of publicity value. Why not endorse a few products and earn some money that way?'

'Are you serious?' Baron stared at the fat man, and Morris reddened beneath the contempt in the cold grey eyes.

'It was a suggestion,' he said hastily. 'I was trying to be helpful.'

'I served the Terran Fleet for fifteen years, ten of them in active service, and all they can do for me is to advise me to peddle my publicity.' Baron snatched up the draft. 'Where do I sign?'

'Here.' Morris watched as the big man scrawled his signature. 'If you are interested I have a friend — '

'No!'

'Be reasonable, Baron. You won't find things too easy in the labour market and you are an untrained man. A few words could earn you thousands of credits, a photograph and a statement even more.' He hesitated. 'Officially I can't appear in this, but if you would like me to arrange things? A percentage, of course, but you wouldn't miss that.' He stared hopefully at the big man. 'What do you think?'

'I think it smells.'

'You may think differently when you're starving in some flophouse,' snapped the fat man. 'Ex-officers are ten a penny outside and you've missed all chance of rehabilitation. Refuse this offer and you'll regret it for the rest of your life.'

'Finished?'

'Don't think you can come back after a few weeks whining for my help.' Morris almost quivered with disappointed anger. 'It will be too late then, you'll be forgotten and the chance missed.' His tone became wheedling. 'Why not, Baron? What's it to you? A few words, a pose or two, and we can both cash in. My friend can arrange everything and there's money all down the line. What do you say?'

'No.'

'You're crazy.' Morris pressed his lips

together like a petulant child as he gathered up the scattered papers and returned them to the file. 'You know the way out.'

'Yes,' said Baron quietly, 'I know the way out.' He rose and stared down at the officer for a moment, his big hands clenched at his sides and his eyes like chips of broken slate.

'That's all, Baron.' Morris didn't look up from where he sat. 'There is no point in your coming back.' His fingers rested on a row of buttons. 'If you want someone to show you the way?'

'Thank you,' gritted Baron tightly. 'For nothing.'

The door jarred on its hinges as he slammed it behind him.

6

A hotel changed the draft, a shabby, run-down building in the old sector of town, still trying to retain a little of its former dignity, but fighting a losing battle with time and neglect. Baron wrinkled his nose at the musty smell seeping from cracked walls and faded carpets, snarling with irritation at the old-fashioned elevator and sly-eyed attendants. A 'boy' showed him to his room, a stooped oldster who would never see forty again, and stood waiting, his hand curved in an age-old gesture. Baron frowned at him.

'What do you want?'

'Everything satisfactory, sir?' The hand became a little more obvious. 'Are you expecting a visitor?'

'Should I be?'

'You could be, sir.' The smile was suggestive. 'Or — '

'No thanks,' Baron remembered civilian customs and flipped a coin into the open palm. 'Know of a good lawyer?'

'Trouble?'

'No.'

'An advisory counsellor then?' The man nodded. 'We have one resident in this hotel. Shall I ask him to call?'

'Yes.' Baron stared distastefully around the sordid room. 'This is a hell of a dump.' He peeled a note from his slender roll. 'Bring me something to drink, something strong.' He remembered a vague promise. 'Tequila, you know it?'

'Certainly.' The stooped old man grinned at the bill in his hand. 'If there is anything else you want, sir, anything, just ring for me.' He nodded, winked, and shuffled from the room. Baron grunted and examined the shower.

He had bathed by the time the messenger returned with a slender, wax-corked bottle and a couple of delicate glasses. Deftly he removed the cork and tilted the bottle, his words muted as he poured out the potent spirit. 'I have informed Mr. Hansard of your wish to see him, sir.' He set down the bottle. 'He will be along within the hour.'

He hesitated. 'Anything further, sir?'

'Do I get any change?'

'Change?' The man raised his eyebrows. 'Liquor is forbidden in the rooms, sir.'

'Forget it.' Baron stared at the man. 'What's your name?'

'Lefty, sir. Just ask for Lefty.'

'Right. Beat it.'

'Yes, sir.'

Alone once more, Baron slumped in a chair and raised the tulip-shaped glass. He stared at the oily contents, and staring let memory carry him back through space and time until, in imagination, he saw a swarthy face, liquid brown eyes lit by inner merriment, a mobile mouth curved in a carefree smile, and flashing white teeth.

'Carlos,' he whispered, and touched the glass to his lips. 'I wish that you could be here now.' He swallowed the tequila.

It surprised him. It seared his throat and tingled his stomach, filled his eyes with tears and doubled him in gasping reaction. Like most spacemen Baron was no stranger to drink, but again, like most men who lived on their reflexes and kept lonely vigil with the silent stars, his drinking was little and his bouts far apart. The potency of the Mexican liquor caught him unawares and numbed him by its impact, but it warmed him, drove some of the misery and chill from his bones, made even the squalor of the cheap hotel room seem more bearable.

He was sipping his third drink when Hansard entered the room.

The advisory counsellor was a thin, hollow-cheeked man with thin grey hair slicked back from a creased forehead, and a nervous, shifty manner of continually dry-washing his hands. His eyes seemed to contain a life of their own and flickered from object to object in ceaseless motion. He smiled as he saw the bottle.

'Ah! Tequila! May I?' He poured a drink without waiting for permission, sniffing the bouquet and sipping with prim precision. 'Good, very good, better with lemon, of course, but a beggar can't be a chooser, can he?' He chuckled with artificial merriment and refilled his glass. 'Our mutual friend tells me that you have a problem. Is that correct?'

'Yes.' Baron coiled the liquor around his tongue and reached for the bottle.

'Then I am the man to help you.' Hansard nodded as he tilted his glass. 'Yes. I am the very man.' He smiled at Baron. 'For a nominal charge I will give you the benefit of my wide knowledge of law, science, politics, and all kindred subjects appertaining to the inevitable conflict attending human affairs.'

'I'm told that you are an advisory counsellor.' Baron glowered at the shifty eyes. 'Credited?'

'Certainly. My bond is with the First National Bank and my certificate of competence was issued by the Law Academy of Illinois. I am fully qualified to sit in advisory judgment on any problem concerned with law. If I say that your case is worth taking to litigation, then you may be assured that it is so. If not, then you save both time and money by consulting me rather than paying the high fees of a lawyer.' He washed his hands with restless motion. 'For a thousand credits — '

'Too much.'

'Indeed?' Hansard frowned. 'For expert advice?' He shrugged and reached for the bottle. 'Between gentlemen, then, and as I am drinking your liquor, shall we say seven-fifty?'

'Let's say five hundred,' suggested Baron, and blinked as he lifted the glass to his lips. 'If I win the case I'll cut you in a couple of thousand.' Rapidly he explained his problem, stressing the fact of his unpaid salary and saying nothing of Morris. Hansard shook his head.

'Sorry, my friend, but you haven't a chance.' He burped and smiled with unabashed apology. 'If you insist on taking the case to the courts you will be stripped of all you own and the results will be the same.'

'Why's that?'

'In law a dead man has no rights. He cannot be penalised, and so, beneath the law, he cannot claim. Only his dependants and creditors can claim, and then only because of personal loss or unfulfilled commitments.' He shrugged. 'You are dead.'

'Like hell I am!'

'In law you are. There is no precedent of a man once dead returning to life, and there was no possibility of error. You were really dead, as stiff as mutton, meat ready for the worms. Sorry.'

'I see.' Baron let liquor slop over his chin. 'There's no hope then?'

'Not unless legislation can be passed through the Senate. You are a precedent, and fresh laws will have to be made to cover any further such cases. That, however, will take time, perhaps decades. I assume that you haven't the money to do the necessary lobbying, bribing, convincing and bringing to bear of pressure in the right places.'

'You assume right.' Tiredly Baron reached for his roll and peeled off five hundred credits. He didn't begrudge the money, it would have cost far more to consult a registered lawyer and the price was cheap for correct advice. Hansard, like many more aspirants after professional status, had found that there wasn't room at the top. To plead at court he had to take expensive examinations, open hard-to-get offices, confine himself to a rigid system of ethics and procedure. The result was the founding of the advisory counsellors, would-be lawyers who just hadn't made the grade and who eked out a living by acting as in-between men, a buffer to the lawyers with their sky-high prices and would-be litigants who wanted to make certain they had a genuine case in law.

Baron knew that he didn't have a chance.

They sat drinking after that, tilting the bottle until it was dry, then sending for more. Strangely, the potent spirit seemed to have no effect on the counsellor. He smiled a little wider, washed his hands a little faster, and his shifty eyes darted at increased speed, but that was all. With Baron it was different.

The alcohol seemed to light tiny fires in his brain. Thoughts coursed through his mind like scurrying rats, clear and bright and wonderful and, as he drank, warm, somehow alien pictures painted themselves against his mental vision. Men, dressed in strange clothing, bearded and weaponed. Women, laughing, screaming, wide-eyed with passion and narrow eyed with hate. The ruby light of smouldering cities and the surging roar of vast seas. Sounds and sights he had never before experienced, tantalising glimpses of a world both familiar and strange, flashing across his mind like the flickering images from a television screen.

Mingled with them were other images, the cold light of the distant stars, the squat form of a cargo vessel exploding into incandescent brilliance, the harsh face of his commanding officer, the greasy features of Morris. He felt rage when he thought of the fat man, a searing, stomach-knotting rage, and he breathed in great rasping gulps, his muscles tensing and his blood pounding through his veins with the sheer desire to rend and tear, rip and destroy, to wallow in blood and —

He grunted as a hand shook his shoulder.

'What's the matter?'

'Are you all right?' Hansard peered at him, his eyes for once no longer flickering from object to object. The thin man seemed worried and his tongue darted, snake-like, over his lower lip.

'Sure I'm all right. Why?'

'You looked — strange.' The counsellor smiled as the big man sat upright in his chair, and his eyes resumed their interrupted flickering.

'Strange?' Baron laughed and tilted a bottle, letting fiery drops fall to his tongue. 'How do you mean?'

'Peculiar, your face seemed — different.' He gestured with his hands. 'I find it impossible to describe. Probably a trick of the light and moving shadow, but you muttered something I couldn't make out what, and seemed to be in pain.'

'I'm in no pain.' Baron rubbed his eyes and stared around the room. Three bottles, all empty, lay on the faded carpet. Spilled liquor had made a sticky puddle on the table and the air was heavy with a peculiar, sickly sweet odour. He sniffed and Hansard twitched thin lips in a smile.

'Anything wrong?'

'That smell. What is it?'

'Tobacco? Surely you have smelt it before?'

'That's not tobacco.' Baron stared at a thick, loosely-rolled cigarette 'Dope!' He glared at the thin man. 'Have I been smoking marijuana?'

'You joined me in a stick of tea,' agreed the counsellor. 'I didn't ask you, but you insisted, and what could I do?' He spread his hands. 'Don't you remember?'

'No.' Baron dropped his throbbing head on to a supporting hand. His mouth seemed to be filled with slime, his eyes hurt and there was a nagging pain at the back of his skull. He felt dirty, ashamed, irritated, and depressed and wished that he were away from all this and back in the cold cleanliness of outer space. He ran his tongue over parched lips. 'What time is it?'

'Almost dawn.' Hansard yawned. 'We had quite a session.'

'Yeah.' The big man stared at the smoke-filled room, the empty bottles and the littered stubs of hand-made cigarettes. 'Get to hell out of here.'

'What!'

'You heard me. Beat it!'

'Really!' The thin man drew himself up

with offended dignity. 'Remember who I am and what I am. I, sir, am a gentleman and I must ask you to address me as such.'

'You're a dirty, dope-peddling shyster,' snarled Baron. 'Now get out of here.'

'You haven't paid me for the tea,' protested the counsellor. 'Those things cost money and I want paying.'

'Do you?' Baron bared his teeth in a humourless smile. Slowly he rose, swaying a little, and glared at Hansard. 'Would you like to collect what I owe?' he said gently, and took a staggering stride forward. 'Would you?'

Hansard gulped and moved hastily towards the door. Standing at the portal he felt safe, and turned to snarl a curse at the big man.

'You dirty moron, I'll make you pay for this, see if I don't. No one takes me for a fool, and I'm damned if you're going to be the first.'

'Get out!' A bottle stood on the floor and Baron reached for it, his big hand snaking around the neck and jerking it level with his shoulder. Swiftly he threw it, the glass spraying in a thousand shards as it smashed with savage violence a foot from the thin man's head. Again he reached for a bottle, this time exploding it into glittering ruin on the closing panel of the door. The third almost buried itself in the plaster of the wall; then, impelled by a savage kick, the small table splintered as it skidded across the floor, a wall mirror collapsed in noisy destruction, and a chair sagged as it yielded to the tearing force of surging muscles.

Baron stared at the ruin, gulping great breaths of smoke-filled air, sweat gleaming on his forehead and his lips writhing back from his teeth as he felt the urge to continue the destruction. He mastered it, fighting with himself until the nails of his fingers dug into his palms, then, staggering clumsily across the floor thrust his head beneath the shower and turned the cold tap full on.

The needle spray of frigid water helped to clear some of the fog and mist from his clouded senses, and stripping he let the shower lash his skin with its icy whips. For a long time he stood there, feeling his flesh grow numb beneath the cold rain, feeling his bones begin to ache from the cold and his teeth chatter in uncontrolled reflex.

When he had dressed and flung wide the smeared windows he was almost himself again. Grimly he counted what money remained in his pockets. Five hundred he had given to Hansard, a hundred in advance for the night's lodging, another hundred for the first bottle of tequila and the rest? He stared down at a crumpled mass of credit notes, smoothing them with his thick fingers and counting them. He should have had about sixteen hundred credits, assuming that he had paid a further hundred credits each for the other two bottles.

He was short by a thousand.

Grimly he stared at his money, feeling anger at having been robbed, but knowing that, he had no right to blame any but himself. A man had to look after what was his, and if he couldn't —

He shrugged and threw himself down on the bed.

7

The next morning he tried to get a job. He joined a long line of waiting men at the gates of a factory, turning away when it was obvious there could be no vacancies. He signed on at three agencies, promising them a full week's pay in return for finding him work, and paying out a hundred-credit registration fee at each office. He borrowed a newspaper and tried to find something in the advertisements and, when it was obvious that he lacked the barest qualifications for even the lowest paid, semi-skilled work, crumpled the sheet in his big hands.

At midday he ate. Stuffing himself full of cheap food at a dingy restaurant, taking double helpings in an effort to ease the mounting pains of hunger leaping within him. From the restaurant he went to the spaceport and, after waiting an hour, managed to get an interview with the labour boss.

'Baron?' The man looked up from his desk. 'I've heard about you; what can I do for you?'

'I want a job.'

'A job.' The labour boss frowned. 'Not much doing here at the moment, in fact I'll have to lay a few off soon.' He stared at the big man. 'You shouldn't have to come here. A man like you should be able to pick up something better than what I can offer.'

'Where?' Baron leaned across the desk. 'I'm not asking for special treatment. All I want is a job, something to give me enough to eat and a place to sleep. I'm a trained pilot, fifteen years with the Terran Fleet, and I can handle any ship in the field.'

'So can any of those.' The man pointed through the windows to where a small group of men worked like Trojans as they unloaded a freighter. 'All ex-officers. All thrown on the labour market at the end of the war. There isn't one of them without ten years space training, and most of them have degrees as well.' He shook his head. 'A few of them found work as freighter pilots when trade resumed with the Martian colonists, but they have all the pilots they need. I'm sorry, Baron, but you see how it is.'

'I'll do anything, skim the repair pits, clean out jets, haul sand for the launching racks. Anything.' He swallowed. 'Give me a chance, can't you?'

'I'd like to, Baron, but — ' The labour boss shook his head. 'Sorry.'

'Are you sure? Isn't there some job I could do? It doesn't matter how dirty or dangerous it is, anything will do. Anything.' He tried to keep the note of pleading from his voice, but it forced its way through. The labour boss looked up from his papers.

'Desperate?'

'Yes.'

'Wife? Children?'

'No, but does that matter?'

'It might.' The man stared at the tips of his fingers. 'There is one job,' he said slowly. 'A nasty, dirty, dangerous job, but if you want it — '

'I'll take it.'

'Take it easy, you haven't heard what it

is yet.' He didn't look at Baron. 'There's a vacancy at the sludge pits. Removing waste radioactives from the power piles.' He shrugged at Baron's instinctive gesture of refusal. 'I told you it was a nasty job. I'm not blaming you for refusing.'

'I haven't refused yet.'

'You can start tomorrow. Five-hour shift at fifty credits the hour and a free meal in the canteen, but I'm warning you, the work is dangerous and the turnover large. We average a complete changeover a month, and,' he looked at his fingers again, 'you can give up any idea of children. The gamma radiation is pretty deadly and you'll be sterile within a week.'

'I'll take it.'

'Are you certain, Baron?' This time the labour boss stared directly at him. 'We usually use criminals; they work off a year of their sentence each week they spend at the pits. I told you it was a nasty job.'

'As bad as that?' Baron shrugged. 'Thanks for the offer, at what time do I start?'

'You said that you were desperate,' reminded the labour boss, 'or I wouldn't have offered it to you.' He wrote on a card. 'Think it over; if you turn it down I'll understand and contact you if anything else turns up.' He handed Baron the card. 'If you decide to start hand this card to the gateman, he will direct you and notify the pit boss.' He hesitated. 'Take your time about it. The card is good for any time tomorrow; we can always fit you in, so there's no need to get here at dawn.' He held out his hand. 'Good luck, Baron, and I hope that you find a better job.'

'Thanks,' said Baron, and meant it. 'I'll sec what I can do.'

From the spaceport he caught a lift back to the city and dropped in a low-rate eating house for a meal. His appetite amazed him; it seemed as if he just couldn't get enough to eat and, as he spooned at the greasy, yeast-culture soup and rough bread, he worried about it. Food wasn't cheap, even the yeast extracts from the culture vats, necessary to augment the natural vegetation, cost almost more than the average man could afford.

And he was eating more than enough for three average men.

After the meal he had a drink, crude rotgut, probably distilled from some illicit still, over a hundred proof alcohol and raw enough to skin the inside of his mouth. It warmed him. With his craving for food he seemed to have acquired a craving for alcohol, strange in a space pilot, worrying also to a man who had always kept himself in the peak of physical condition. Thinking about it increased the craving, and he had another drink, then a third, feeling the little fires light in his brain, feeling too his depression and worry fall away like a tattered garment.

When he left the place he was almost cheerful.

The route back to the hotel led past the towering building of the Terran Fleet and, acting on impulse, he stepped inside. A uniformed private looked up from where he sat, a gaudy comic on his lap, and frowned in irritation at being disturbed.

'Yes?'

'I want to enlist.'

'Do you?' The man yawned. 'Why'

'That's my business. Where's the recruiting officer?'

'There isn't one.'

'What are you talking about? There must be.'

'Why must there be?' The man stretched with languid indifference. 'The war's over. We don't need any more men now.' He yawned again. 'Thanks for coming, try again when the next war is declared.'

Before Baron had turned away he was deep in his comic, chuckling over the antics of painted fools in a painted world.

Back at the hotel trouble waited. It came forward in the guise of a tight-mouthed man, his synthosilk betraying his wealth, his narrowed eyes, his bitter soul. Behind him crowded the stooped figure of Lefty, and behind him, his thin face triumphant, Hansard pressed forward to see the fun.

'Baron?' The tight-mouthed man rapped the word as if he were firing a bullet. 'I'm

Carson, I own this hotel.'

'So what?'

'So you owe me two thousand credits damage.' He held out his hand, palm upwards. 'Give.'

'Like hell!' Frustration and anger sharpened the big man's voice. 'Take it out of the thousand your 'boy' lifted from me last night.'

'I want that money, Baron.'

'If you find it you can have it.' Bitterness made his voice harsh and he felt anger tense his muscles. 'I haven't got two thousand or anything like it.'

'So?' The narrowed eyes didn't change expression. 'Can you get it?'

'Maybe.'

'Where from?'

'That's my business.'

'And mine.' Carson stared at the stooped figure of Lefty. 'Did you take his money?'

'No.'

'He's lying,' snapped Baron contemptuously. 'He must have taken it; if he didn't then that dope-pedlar must have done.'

'What?' Something flickered in the cold eyes. 'What did you call him?'

'He's lying, Carson.' Hansard thrust his thin body forward, his hand clutching at a synthosilk arm. 'Pay no attention.'

'Shut up, you fool.' Abruptly Carson's manner changed. He smiled, brushing off the hand on his arm, and jerked his head towards the big man. 'Let's talk this over. Drink?'

'Thanks.'

'Right. Lefty, a couple of bottles in this gentleman's room.' He smiled at Baron. 'If you will lead the way?'

The room had been tidied, the ruin removed and the table replaced. Carson sat down, his cold eyes thoughtful. As Lefty set down the bottles he jerked his head in dismissal. Hansard stretched out a thin hand and poured out drinks.

'You're a strange man, Baron.' Carson lifted his glass and stared at his brandy. 'Hansard has told me about you.'

'Yes?'

'You mentioned something downstairs. What do you know?'

'Nothing.'

'Must I refresh your memory?' Something of the tiger peered through the narrowed eyes. 'You can speak freely here, you could almost call us — friends?'

'Well — friend,' said Baron with heavy sarcasm, 'I know that this hotel is a dump. At a hundred credits a day you wouldn't get a self-respecting rat to sleep here. So there must be a reason for the high prices, and that reason is partly concerned with our friend's habit of smoking reefers and passing them around to casual guests. What was he after? A new addict?'

'I offered you a smoke from pure friendship,' muttered Hansard. 'A gesture to a drinking companion.'

'A gesture for which you wanted payment.' Baron shrugged. 'Don't get me wrong, personally I don't give a damn what you do, but just keep off my neck, will you?'

'You were careless, Hansard.' Carson almost purred as he sipped his brandy. 'This man could have been a stooge from the police. You were lucky.' He handed Baron a drink and watched as the big man drained the glass at a single gulp. 'You drink deep, my friend.'

'So what?'

'Nothing. Are you working?'

'I've a job to go to.'

'Good.' Carson rose. 'You may stay here if you wish.' A smile curved the corners of his humourless mouth. 'Window dressing shall we say? Just see nothing, hear nothing, and remember to keep your mouth shut.'

'And the rates?' Baron reached for the bottle.

'Two hundred a week — on the nail.'

'Fair enough.' The big man smiled as he hefted the one full and one partly opened bottle. 'Goodnight.'

He was too busy drinking to notice when they left.

The next day he started work. Dressed in thick, cumbersome, anti-radiation armour he sweated in the sludge pits as he cleaned the waste radioactives from the rocket power piles. The work was hard, grappling with tongs almost as heavy as he could lift, shifting weight at odd angles, trying not to think of the invisible death permeating the entire area from the spilled radioactives. With him worked criminal scum, desperate men glad of the chance to work off a few years of their sentences, and yet trying their best to dodge what could not be avoided. It could not be done. The sludge had to be taken from the pile, shifted to the disposal containers and the containers themselves loaded into heavy, cadmium and lead-sheathed transports. Baron had the job of loading, and his muscles cracked as he heaved the heavy bins into position.

Once a day he ate free at the spaceport canteen, eating enormous quantities of food, stuffing himself against the too frequent hunger tearing at his vitals. After his five-hour shift, when he had washed and rubbed anti-radiation salve into his skin, he went to the poorest section of the city and there drank the crudest, cheapest liquor obtainable. Life narrowed to work, eating and drinking, dream-haunted nightmares, and work again. The alcohol seemed to keep alight the tiny fires within his skull, and though he never seemed to get helplessly drunk yet he was never wholly sober. The craving for alcohol, like the insatiable craving for food, was so inexplicable that he had long since stopped worrying about it.

After a month he lost his job.

He awoke the morning after, his mouth furry with the familiar after-effects of too much liquor, and sat for a long time on the edge of his bed, head in his hands, trying to clear the mist away from his mind. Light seeped through the dirty windows and he squinted at it, staring at it as at something totally unrecognisable, then tiredly he heaved himself up from the bed and stepped into the shower.

He stood for a long time in the cold spray, letting the water cool his feverish body, feeling it drum against his skull and wash across his face. Soaping himself well he rubbed the lather into bulging muscles and barrel chest, rubbing his fingers through the thick hair matting his body and massaging his limbs with the milk-white foam. Soaped, he let the stream of ice-cold water flush him clean, then stepped from the shower on to the mat, slapping at the switch of an air dryer as he stood before the grill. Warm blasts played around his naked body and, while waiting to be dried, he stared thoughtfully at his reflection in a mirror hung against the wall.

For a moment he imagined that he stared at a stranger. A big man, thick-set, with smoothly sloping shoulders and tremendous biceps. The neck was a tree-like column, the jaw massive, the cheekbones prominent and the ridge of bone above the eyes lowering from the sloping forehead. Only the eyes remained the same, cold and grey, bloodshot now, but still hard and bleak in their sockets. The eyes and the scar that writhed over his left cheek and puckered his lips into a sneer. Stubble coated his lips and chin, and his cropped hair was a tousled mess. He grimaced and the illusion was broken, and as he irritably covered the stubble with depilatory cream and wiped both cream and hairs off on a paper towel it vanished still more. Hair oil added sheen and order to his tousled mess, self-acting paste removed the stains from his once-white teeth, and astringent lotion made his cheeks glow with artificial health.

He had just finished dressing when the knock came at the door.

'Who is it?' He glowered as the panel swung wide and he saw the thin face of the counsellor. 'You! What do you want?'

'Take it easy, Baron, I'm here to help.' The thin man slipped through the open door, and another man, a dark-skinned Eurasian, followed silently after. Both men sat on the edge of the sofa, and Hansard began talking before the big man could throw them out.

'You're in a spot, Baron, I know it and there's no sense in you acting otherwise. You lost your job yesterday didn't you?'

'How did you know?'

'A month is all they let you work at the sludge pits, and they're running things fine even then.' The counsellor smiled as his eyes flickered over the room. 'You may not realise it, Baron, but you're a sick man. Those radiations haven't done you any good and you'll need plenty of rest and good food before you can think of work again.'

'So what?'

'So there's rent to pay and food to buy, and liquor, you need plenty of liquor, don't you, Baron? Carson won't let you owe much rent and, believe me, Carson isn't a man to forgive. He's got a few goons to take care of his dirty work, nasty types with knives and the willingness to use them. He wants paying on the nail, Baron.'

'I can pay him.'

'Can you? For how long? A week? Two weeks? A month even? And after that?' Hansard smiled. 'You could move, of course, live in a bug-ridden flop house down among the ruins, but would you like that, Baron? A man like you, an ex-officer, a man used to the cleanliness of space?' He dry-washed his hands. 'I think not, Baron.'

'What are you after?' Baron glared distastefully at the olive-skinned man with the ridiculous turban set with an obviously false gem. 'Who is this clown?'

'He could be your friend, Baron. A very

good friend. He is a Guru, a teacher, and — but there! He can tell you himself.'

'I'm not interested.'

'No?' Hansard nudged the Guru, who silently produced a bottle of liquor. 'Now are you interested?'

'Do you take me for a drunk?' Baron glared at the thin man, muscles knotting along the line of his jaw and his hands tightening into fists. 'Get out!'

'I meant no harm!' Hansard recoiled on the dingy sofa. 'A mere peace offering, a token of my regard, a civilised custom over which we could have a friendly discussion.'

'You tried to bribe me with your stinking liquor.' Anger sent little tremors racing through his muscles. 'You think that a bottle can make me behave, that I would grovel like a dog at your feet for the sake of rotgut poison. Hell! Have I sunk so low?'

'A moment, my friend.' The dark man spoke, and his voice was pure melody. 'You are letting the illusion blind you to the reality. There is no harm in the giving or the accepting of gifts. The wine?' He shrugged and deliberately thrust it aside. 'The wine is nothing, if it will please you it can be broken and be as if it never was. It was not for that I came.'

'Then get out.'

'Take it easy, Baron.' Sweat glistened on the thin man's forehead. 'At least listen to what he has to say.'

'A thousand credits if you will but listen.' The Guru calmly peeled the sum off a thick wad. 'A second thousand if you will join my friend in a glass of wine. A third thousand if you will promise not to lose your temper again.' He smiled like some Eastern god, over the little heap of notes. 'Well?'

'It's a deal.' Baron scooped up the money and thrust the notes into his pocket. Hansard grinned, sweating like a man just reprieved from the gallows, and his thin hands trembled as he opened the brandy. A glass rested on the floor, dusty and stained with old liquor. He washed it in the shower, rinsed a water glass, and set them both on the small table, filling them with the golden promise of heaven on earth. Glass clicked as he rattled it against his teeth, and brandy rilled down his chin. He grunted as he set down the empty tumbler.

'Go ahead, Guru, he's listening.'

'First, let me explain that I am the spiritual head and temporal adviser of the sect known as the Electro-Mechanists.' The Guru bent his head as if in homage as he spoke the words. 'My flock, while not large, is select and extremely influential, an elite of the mass, a group who seek to find the true path through the undoubted manifestations of the Electro-Mechanist approach to the infinite. You have heard of us, perhaps?'

'No.'

'Then perhaps I should explain that our tenets are that the Universe is a materialistic entity governed by the ebb and pulse of the electro-magnetic waves, and ruled over by the One. Life is explained in the terms of the laboratory, but the hereafter is still open to both proof and doubt. We hold that the ego is but part of an infinite reservoir of intelligence, that after death we return to the Mother Flow and there mingle with all those who have been and who ever will be.' He paused. 'You follow me?'

'No.'

'Naturally my explanation is poor. I have hardly the time to show you the significance of the symbols and phenomena attendant to the Prime Function, but it must suffice. However, let it remain that after death the individual does not die but merely remerges with the One, there to experience all the joys and passions of all those who have ever lived, sharing and vibrating to all other lives, retaining individual awareness, and yet capable of complete merging with all forms of life in the entire Universe at will, either as spectators or as temporary owners of illusion.'

'Illusion?'

'Certainly. All this, our bodies, this world, is nothing but illusion. But to continue. After death the ego, as I have explained, returns to the One, there to enjoy all until such time as rebirth or, as we say, re-entrance into illusion is desired. This necessitates a mental blankness of past experience and knowledge in order to complete the illusion, which can only survive while it is thought to be real.'

'Nice racket.' Baron stared at his brandy, fighting the desire to empty the glass, and forcing himself to put it down untouched. 'It answers almost everything. Even to the lack of real knowledge of this so-called 'One'.' He nodded. 'Very nice. Did you dream it up or can anyone join in?'

'I am proud to be the instigator and leader of the sect,' said the Eurasian gravely. 'The Electro-Mechanistic doctrine embraces both old superstition and modern discovery. It is the answer to all.'

'Congratulations. Where do I come in?'

'I would have thought,' said the dark man quietly, 'that would have been obvious to a person of even average intelligence.'

'Yeah.' Baron's hand moved from table to mouth and back again, the empty glass ringing on the stained wood as he set it down. 'Now I get it.'

'Every religion needs at least one miracle,' murmured the Guru smoothly. 'Faith is so rarely sufficient for the weak illusion which is human frailty.' He spread his hands and smiled as if forgiving all the sins of the world. 'A few waverers, a few doubters, a few who decry the wisdom of the ancients — '

'A few suckers who don't like being plucked?' Baron stared sombrely at his glass. 'Shall we cut the nonsense and talk English? I'm not one of those fat fools you soft-soap with jargon. I've got more to do with my time than kid myself I'm one of the elite.' He reached for the bottle and looked at the Eurasian over the rim of his brimming glass. 'How much?'

'A man of perception.' The Guru nodded. 'A man with whom I like to deal.' He smiled with a flash of too-white teeth, the smile dying like the fire of a blown match. 'You understand what it is you have to do? Not that I ask you for anything but the truth, you understand, but it is possible that you carry a message of tremendous importance and it is my duty to see that your message reaches the ears of the understanding.' He leaned forward, the tips of his slender, almost fragile fingers rested lightly on his knees. 'You follow?'

'I follow,' said Baron thickly. 'A man who died and returned to life again.' His voice deepened with self-disgusted irony. 'For five years I was dead, rejoined with the One, and when illusion called to me I re-entered, full grown and with unimpaired memory. I am the living proof that the Electro-Mechanist doctrine is the true path to reality, the only proof, the accidental messenger from the hereafter.'

'Exactly. Naturally there will be a little briefing, and the groundwork will have to be prepared, but your task will be simple.' He stared at the big man. 'One other thing. It would not be wise to do other than directed, and I take you for a wise man.'

'Don't worry, I won't try to snatch your glory, your pigeons are safe from me.' Baron gulped the smooth brandy. 'How much?'

'For a message of such import I do not consider fifty thousand credits to be too high a price.'

'Fifty thousand?' Baron shrugged. 'Chicken

feed! Once I tell those fat matrons what they've got to look forward to if they follow the path donations will flow in like rain. Think again, Guru, I'm not that cheap.'

'No?' Eyes of liquid jet glanced at the half-empty bottle. 'Perhaps not. One hundred thousand then, ten thousand a week for ten weeks. I doubt if you will be needed after that.'

'What do I do then, return to the One?' Baron grinned without humour. 'Don't try anything clever, Guru. Pay me and I'm satisfied, try a second miracle and I'm liable to get annoyed.'

'There need be no fear on that account.'

'I hope not. Shall we say fifty now and fifty after I've given the message?'

'I prefer to give you five thousand now, fifty thousand after the message and the remainder when our association is ended.'

'Ten down, ten a week, and one hundred thousand when, as you say, our association is ended.' Baron slammed the bottle on to the table. 'No arguing. You've heard my price. Take it or leave it.'

'You are a hard man, Captain Baron.'

'Miracles come dear, my friend. Pay me and get out!'

He waited until the Eurasian counted out a sheaf of notes, sitting silent and still as both men rose and left the room, Hansard's promise to return and act as intermediary ringing like an unclean promise in his ears. He sat until the light began to fade through the dirty windows, staring at the bottle, wondering what had happened to him, and not liking what he thought about.

The golden sheen of the brandy triggered an automatic response and he picked up the bottle, poured a glass full of the lambent fluid and hesitated, the bottle still poised in his hand.

Savagely he flung it against the wall.

8

In the brilliant circle of light the stained culture of Streptococci looked like a collection of beads strung together in writing chains. Around them the dark bulks of leucocytes seemed ugly and awkward in comparison to the tiny bacteria, small and graceful in their deadly presence in the blood sample. Whitney stared at them, his eyes firm against the rubber-mounted eyepieces of the twin-barrelled three-dimensional microscope and, with the skill of long practice, his right hand made rapid, unseen notes. He looked up as Le Maitre entered the laboratory.

'Sorry to disturb you,' said the old man. 'I know how it is when research is interrupted, but we have a visitor.'

'A visitor?' Whitney snapped off the powerful microscope light and replaced the slide back into its container. 'Baron?'

'A pity.' The young man blinked hard,

closing his eyes and moistening the balls with rapid motions of his eyelids as he helped them recover from the strain of recent concentration. 'Who then?'

'Inspector McMillan, a policeman from Greater New York.' The old man led the way into the corridor. 'He arrived on the mid-shift rocket and seems in a hurry to see you.'

'Why me?'

'Well, both of us then.' Le Maitre slid aside a panel. 'You can ask the questions yourself, the inspector is waiting for us in the recreation room.'

McMillan was a big, almost bulky man with sharp blue eyes and sparse brown hair. He wore his trim uniform of blue and scarlet as if born to it, and he wasted no time

'Doctor Whitney?'

'Yes?'

'My apologies for disturbing your work, doctor, but I must catch the next rocket to Earth and there isn't too much time.' He pulled a thick sheaf of papers from a briefcase. 'To be frank I've the feeling that this trip will be wasted effort, but in my business no lead, no matter how remote or absurd looking, can be ignored.' He glanced at the two men. 'Have you read the newspapers or heard newscasts recently?'

'I haven't,' said Whitney, and glanced at the old doctor. Le Maitrc shook his head.

'Nor I, there is too much to do here, too many scientific papers to catch up with.' He grunted as he sat down 'Why do you ask?'

'You'd better read this, it will save time.' The inspector threw a lurid-headlined paper on to the table, and Whitney pursed his lips as he scanned the brief details.

'What has this to do with us?'

'Perhaps nothing.' The inspector shrugged as he replaced the paper in his briefcase. 'The point is this. We know that Baron got mixed up with this cult, this pseudo-religion calling themselves the Electro-Mechanists, and we know that he worked with an Eurasian known as the Guru, but with a rather less exotic name in our files. Incidentally, he was arrested a couple of years ago for trying to persuade a woman to sign big cheques over to him while beneath the influence of hypnotism. Before that he dabbled in dope, a little opium and some marijuana, even touched cocaine, I believe, but we never had proof of that. As I said, we know that Baron was mixed up with him. You can guess why?'

'Yes,' said Whitney disgustedly. 'As the resurrected man he would be in a perfect position to persuade certain fools of the truth of the hereafter.'

'Exactly. That isn't important. There is no crime in organising a religion, and if people are stupid enough to believe a lot of nonsense, that is up to them.' The inspector hesitated. 'The only thing is — the Guru was murdered.'

'Murdered?'

'Yes. We found his body a few hours ago. As yet the discovery has been kept quiet, no need to warn the rats that we're after them. His body was found in the ruined section of the old city, the part near the river, you know. He hadn't died too easily. The major cause of death was a broken neck, hut he had been severely handled and beaten up. His face was practically unrecognisable, we identified him from fingerprints, and he had every appearance of having been mauled by a wild animal,'

'I see.' Le Maitre glanced at the young man, then back to the inspector. 'But what has this to do with us?'

'I'm worried about the identity of the man calling himself Baron,' admitted the policeman. 'I have several eye-witness descriptions and, of course, his record with the Terran Fleet, and that's why I'm here.'

'Indeed?' Le Maitre shrugged. 'I still don't see — '

'The descriptions do not match, doctor.' McMillan leaned forward as he spoke. 'According to the official records Baron was a well-built man but not overly muscular. Space pilots seldom are, the very nature of their work precludes too much bulky muscular development. Also, the record gives Baron's weight at eighty-three kilos, but the witnesses swear to the fact that the man who must have murdered the Guru was at least ninety-five. That's quite a bit of difference, and that isn't all.' He reached again into the brief-case. 'Is this the man you know as Baron?'

Whitney took the full plate, full colour photograph, and both he and Le Maitre stared at the scene. It showed a small group of men and women, one, obviously the Guru, dressed in dark brown synthosilk and wearing a white, gem-adorned turban. Next to him stood a big man, and Whitney stared at him, passed on, frowned as he looked at him again, then glanced at the inspector.

'Is this the man you mean?'

'Yes.'

'That isn't Baron,' said Le Maitre decisively. He gave a dry chuckle. 'I had the best opportunity in the world to examine the man, we both did, and they are not the same.'

'Are you certain?' McMillan looked at the young doctor. Whitney slowly shook his head.

'I don't know,' he said quietly. 'At first glance I should say no, but — '

'You are foolish, my boy,' said the old man impatiently. 'They are nowhere near alike.'

'I wouldn't say that, Le Maitre. There is a certain similarity — ' Whitney looked at the inspector. 'Can't you make certain by fingerprints? Baron's must be on file.'

'They are, and we can't.' McMillan shrugged. 'Someone beat us to it. He lived in a cheap hotel down by the ruins, a sleazy place used mostly by petty crooks and minor criminals. We know of it, but there isn't any point in closing it down, the rats would only find some other bolthole, and it's better to know where to find them in case of need. As soon as the body was discovered we searched the place. No results. The room and everything he might have left his prints on had been cleaned.' He sighed. 'Believe it or not that photograph is the only thing we have to work on.'

'Isn't it enough?'

'Hardly. The ruins are full of down-and-outs, petty thieves, touts, hangers-on, beggars, the homeless and unwanted. They stick together against the law, and trying to find someone is hopeless. If we knew for certain just what the man looked like, could circulate his prints and

De Witt details for recognition, it would only be a matter of time, but until we know whether or not it is Baron we want, or merely someone who borrowed his name, we can't do much in the way of an extensive search.' He sighed. 'I'd hoped that perhaps you could help me, but it seems that I've wasted my time.'

'Perhaps not.' Whitney gestured with the photograph. 'Do you mind if I have an enlargement made? I want to blow up the features of this man.'

'Go ahead.' The inspector glanced at his wristwatch. 'How long will it take?'

'Not long.' Whitney rose and headed towards the door. 'I'll be back as fast as I can.'

He was back minutes later with an enlargement of the suspected man in his hand. Carefully he spread it on the table.

'The lab boys did what they could. Luckily the original focus was remarkably sharp. We managed to blow it up quite a bit before running into granular trouble.' He stared down at the enlarged head and shoulders. 'On which cheek did Baron have a scar?'

'The left, I think.' Le Maitre frowned as he tried to remember. 'I could make certain from the files.'

'Never mind. I remember now, it was the left cheek.'

Whitney pursed his lips as he stared at the print. 'No sign of a scar here. I — ' He broke off, narrowing his eyes as he stared at the oddly-shaped skull formation. From a drawer he took a magnifying glass and held it over the exposed left cheek of the man in the photograph. 'Look. Apparently there isn't a scar, it doesn't even show on the enlargement, but see?' His finger traced a wavering line across the print. 'The enlargement has brought it out, a difference in the light intensity from the skin surface. See?'

'What does that mean? Plastic surgery?'

'Not necessarily, inspector. Skin dressing could have disguised the scar, or if it had healed in a thin line the result would be the same.'

'Healed?' Le Maitre snorted. 'Impossible!'

'Perhaps.' Whitney stared thoughtfully at the print. 'You know, Le Maitre, the longer I look at this the more convinced I am that he is Baron. The colouring of the eyes is the same, that cold, hard, slate-like grey. The mouth, the scar, if it is a scar, and the shape of the hair. All the same.'

'You are a fool,' said Le Maitre impatiently. 'That man cannot be Baron. Wait, I will prove it.' Before they could stop him he had ran from the room, blue eyes snapping with exasperation, and when he returned he carried a bulky file.

'Now see.' He jerked it open and spilled photographs onto the table. 'Baron when rescued. Baron when stripped and ready for the immersion vat. Baron after being revived. Baron during exercise and Baron during examination prior to leaving for Earth.' He snorted as he stirred the prints with the tip of his finger. 'Do any of them look like your mysterious man?'

'No,' admitted the young doctor. He rifled the prints, and took one showing head and shoulders in approximately the same position as that of the enlargement. 'Wait!'

'You've found something?' McMillan

leaned forward, his eyes eager. 'Are they the same? Is it Baron we want?'

'I'm not sure.' Whitney looked at the old man. 'What do you think?' His finger tapped alternately on the print and the enlargement. 'See? The occipital region, the frontal arch, the lower mandible and the nose. Especially the nose. Couple that with the position of the cheekbones, the upper mandible, the ear lobes and the size and colouring of the eyes, and what do you get?'

'Impossible!' Le Maitre snatched at the photograph and scanned it with his blue eyes wide in amazement. 'A comparison slide would eliminate all doubt, but Whitney, the thing is incredible!'

'Maybe, but I think that it's happened.' Neither man bothered to explain what they were talking about to the inspector. He called out as Whitney left the room carrying both enlargement and photo-graph.

'What's going on here? I've a rocket to catch, remember, and I can't spare too much time.'

'Forget your stupid rocket,' snapped Le

Maitre. 'We must be certain of this thing. If what my young friend suspects is true, then it is the most remarkable scientific discovery ever made.' He hurried from the room.

McMillan shrugged and settled down to wait.

It took over an hour to make the comparison slide, and long before it was ready Le Maitre was trembling with impatience. Tensely he watched the young doctor slip it into the machine, dimming the lights and leaning forward as he adjusted the fine controls. On a screen two images sharpened into focus, the head and shoulders of a man, one taken from the photograph in the file, the other from the print brought by the inspector. Both were exactly to the same scale, and the light density of either could be adjusted at will.

'Now,' said Whitney tensely. 'If I'm right, overlapping the prints will prove it.' He turned a control and the prints blurred, merged, and sharpened to focus again. Overlapping the mystery man the print of Baron showed white against a

149

black background and, as Whitney adjusted the Vernier controls, parts of the white print fitted exactly against the black.

'That proves it,' said Le Maitre dully. 'The brain areas correspond to within a millimetre and the occipital regions are the same. The frontal features are different, but that — '

'They are the same man.' Whitney drew in his breath with a soft inhalation. 'Incredible! And yet true, the slides prove it.'

'But how?'

'Retrogression.' Whitney switched off the projector. 'It has been known to a limited extent before, certain diseases thicken bone and alter the features, but I've never heard of anything like this. Baron was in perfect health when he left us a few months ago. The change seems fantastic, unbelievable, it is against all medical teaching.' He shook his head. 'Even now I can't accept it.'

'It is a fact.' Now that he was convinced, the old doctor had no time for doubts. 'We can rule out disease, Baron didn't have any and, besides, the change has occurred too fast for that.' He looked at the young doctor. 'That leaves us with but one possible answer.'

'The neuron surgery?' Whitney nodded. 'I'd thought of that. Bypassing the censor did more than we suspected. It not only eliminated the barrier between the conscious and subconscious, cut away the restraining influence between thought and action, but my interference resulted in the entire 'dead' area of the brain being placed in free contact with the higher centres. But who could have guessed it would lead to this?'

'We must face facts,' said Le Maitre sternly. 'This is an opportunity not to be missed. The man must be found, held, studied. Who knows what questions of evolution may be answered by careful observation.'

'What of McMillan?'

'The policeman? He must be told. There must be no danger of Baron being shot by some stupid fool in the line of so-called duty.'

'Yes. He isn't responsible, of course, he probably doesn't even know what happened to him.' He shuddered. 'Let's tell the inspector.'

McMillan heard the news with a cold, professional indifference that almost drove Le Maitre to a frenzy. He stormed with impatience as he tried to explain, but the more he tried the more he lost himself in highly technical jargon, and the more he lost himself the more icy McMillan became.

'Please, doctor,' he said quietly. 'Are you trying to tell me that you have decided the print I brought with me is a photograph of Baron?'

'I am.'

'Thank you. Now what else were you trying to say?'

'I can explain.' Whitney stepped forward and pushed the stuttering doctor into a chair. 'To begin with let me make it clear that Baron is not responsible for anything he may have done or may do in the future. While he was here, during the resuscitation process I had to operate on his brain. In short I cut out the censor, the part of the brain that, in brief, could be said to contain the moral centre. I also opened neuron paths from the frontal lobes to the occipital zone. I must admit that, at the time, I didn't know what I was doing.'

'Unethical surgery, doctor?'

'No. The man was dead, what I did was done in an effort to revive him.'

'I see. Continue, please.'

'The result was to merge the brain into a composite whole, and, remember this, McMillan, the conscious portion of the brain is but one tenth of the entire cortex.' Whitney sighed. 'We don't really know what the subconscious is. We can only guess why we only use one tenth of our brain and what the other nine tenths are for. Now, because of what has happened, I think we have found the answer.' He sat down and looked at the inspector. 'We are animals, McMillan. You and I and all humanity are animals that have risen by evolution or mutation from beasts. We are the descendants of primeval man, the Cro-Magnon, the Neanderthal, the Peking, and from those before them. We don't know just what our distant ancestors looked like, we can only guess, but we have come from them in a straight line of unbroken generations.'

'Obviously, otherwise we wouldn't be here.'

'Yes.' Whitney paused, seeking the words, which, while not too technical, yet would explain just what he feared had happened. 'When you mix one tenth of a thing with nine tenths of something else, the nine tenths will be dominant. If the thing you mix is something like strepto-cocci with leucocytes then the streptococci will dominate the leucocytes and the patient will die. If you could mix the past and the present then the past will dominate over the present.' He looked helplessly at the inspector. 'My analogies are bad, I know, but they will serve to point out what I mean. You see, the 'dead' areas of the brain contain all the racial traits and memo-ries. They contain all the data accumulated by generations, and that data is stored in what we call the subconscious. Now, when I operated and merged the two sections of the brain together, all that preponderance of racial memory mingled with the smaller portion of present-day fact. In other words, I mixed the past with the present — *and the past won*!'

He paused then, watching the blank expression on the inspector's face give way to reluctant understanding, and before McMillan had a chance to voice his doubts he piled on the evidence.

'We know that the human body, while as a foetus, goes through the entire life-cycle while within the womb. The unborn child passes through the gill stage, betrays simian characteristics, and even has a tail. Only during the last few months of gestation can it really be called human. If you have ever seen a newborn, premature baby, you will know what I mean. What is happening to Baron is the reverse of that. The accumulated racial 'memories', for want of a better word, are influencing both his mind and his body. Literally, he is retrogressing down the evolutionary scale.'

'I don't believe it!' McMillan glared his protest. 'I can understand how your meddling with his brain may have sent him off the rails, but all this other talk — ' He snorted. 'It's fantastic!'

'I agree with you, but it happens to be the truth.' Whitney pointed to the comparison slide. 'Look! Notice how the features are changing. The thickening of the jaw, of the ridge of bone above the eyes, the apparently sloping skull due to the aggravated weight of the frontal arch. See how the cheekbones have protruded so as to protect the eyes. Even the nose has flattened a little, not much, but it is there, and the upper jaw — ' He slapped down the slide. 'Do you want to know where to see another such man? I can tell you, McMillan. You can see just such features in any natural history museum. I tell you that Baron is changing!'

'But how? A man's body can't change like that. It's impossible!'

'Not impossible,' snapped Le Maitre, 'merely improbable, there is an important scientific difference.'

'You underrate the power of the mind,' said Whitney tiredly. 'We have known for a long time that illness can be directly caused by a peculiar mental state. If a man really believes that he is ill, then he will be ill, and his illness will be due solely to his mental condition. Psychosomatics has passed from the theoretical stage and is common therapy now. Before even a start can be made to cure stomach ulcers, asthma, hysterical blindness or paralysis, the mind must be healed of false convictions, opposed drives, and self-destructive tendencies. It is cold fact that the mind is master of the body.' He looked at the inspector. 'Surely you have heard of people under hypnosis who can cut themselves and not bleed? Injure themselves and not suffer? Even the wounds received in such a condition can be made to heal with fantastic speed. That is further evidence of the power of the mind over the body. There are others, the ability of certain trained minds to go into a state of catalepsy, or of altering their heartbeat, a thing impossible to the average person. No, inspector, we have proof that such a thing can, and does, happen.'

'I'll take your word for it, but what about Baron? His case is a little different to those you have mentioned.'

'Only in degree.' Whitney frowned. 'It is the time element that is worrying me. If only he had stayed here, or even reported to a hospital on Earth, we could have spotted the change and maybe have done something for him.'

'Just as long as I know who we're looking for.' McMillan rose to his feet and glanced again at his wristwatch. 'I'll broadcast the De Witt recognition factors and alert the entire force. He won't get away.'

'I don't want him harmed, inspector.'

'Don't you?' McMillan stared at the young man. 'Don't you think that I'm the best judge of that?'

'No.'

'Why not?'

'Your job is to catch a man suspected of murder, and I've no doubt that you do the job well, but I know the police and I know how they operate. Baron is a frightened man. He won't stop when challenged. Fear will make him run, and your men are trained to shoot at any man running from a command to halt. I don't want Baron shot.'

'Neither do I,' admitted McMillan. 'Even if he did kill the Guru, and there's not much doubt about it now, I can realise that he may not be responsible for his actions.' He hesitated. 'This change you've talked about. As far as I can see it has altered him quite a bit already. How far will it go?'

'I don't know.' Whitney glanced at the old man, and Le Maitre shook his head.

'It will accelerate, that I can tell you, but the rate of change is dependent on so many factors. Without data it is impossible to say.'

'Impossible, doctor — or improbable?' McMillan smiled at the old man. 'I can supply you with some data if that's what you want. We've managed to fill in the gaps on Baron, it was just that I didn't want to waste time chasing the wrong man.' He took a sheet of paper from his briefcase. 'From the start he seems to have hit the bottle pretty heavily. He — '

'What!' Whitney snatched at the paper. 'Alcohol! Le Maitre! There's the answer!'

'The synapses?' The old man nodded. 'It could be.'

'Alcohol is a depressant,' explained Whitney to the inspector. 'It lowers the speed of the synapses, the jumping of electrical potential from one nerve ending to another, and from one cell to another. In short, it reduces the efficiency of the higher centres, the conscious mind, and allows the subconscious to become slightly more dominant than normal.' He looked at Le Maitre. 'That must have been the trigger that started the whole thing. Once the lower centres of the brain achieved dominance, and they could because of the lack of a censor and the new paths opened by neuron surgery, then the change must have started almost at once.' He slammed his right fist into his left palm. 'The fool! Why did he have to drink?'

'Maybe he was thirsty?' McMillan retrieved his crumpled sheet of paper. 'Anyway, after trying to get a job he finally managed to get a place in the sludge pits at the spaceport.'

'Radiation,' groaned Whitney. 'Hell! It was inevitable. What fools we were not to have guessed.' He looked at the inspector. 'I suppose that he ate a great deal as well?'

'Yes, how did you know? The spaceport

canteen reported that he ate like a starving man.'

'Naturally, he needed the food to supply energy for his changing metabolism. Once his body began to alter he would literally be burning his energy at tremendous speed. The alcohol would supply some of it, but he would need protein for new tissue.' Whitney glowered down at the floor. 'What a chance! Missed because we were too blind to see what we had done.' He stared at McMillan. 'I'm coming to Earth with you.'

'That will hardly be necessary, doctor. I assure you that we can manage.'

'Can you?' Grim humour curved the young man's mouth. 'Do you know what you are looking for?'

'Baron, or a man with his fingerprints. Don't worry, we'll find him.'

'I doubt it. Haven't you realised yet what we have been telling you? The man is changing, all of him, every cell and particle. His fingerprints even. His face. His bone structure. Your men could pass him a thousand times and never recognise him for what he is. Look at those photographs! You can see what alteration has taken place within a few weeks. How long is it since that man, that Guru, was killed?'

'About ten days.'

'There you are then. In ten days at the rate he is retrogressing Baron would be unrecognisable to any but an expert.' He stared at the policeman. 'And there's another reason.'

'Yes?'

'I want to be there — just in case.'

'Have it your own way then, doctor, but don't step on my feet. As far as I'm concerned Baron is still a murderer, and he's got to be caught.'

'Yes,' whispered Whitney sickly. 'He's got to be caught — but not because you think he's killed a man.'

'No?'

'No. He's got to be caught because I shudder to think what might happen if one of our distant ancestors were to walk the streets of a modern city. A creature with the warped intelligence of a man and all the raw, primitive emotion of a beast. Now do you understand?'

'Yes,' said McMillan quietly. 'I think I do.'

He was almost running as he left the room, heading for the rocket to take him and Whitney down to Earth.

9

The crowd roared. The sound of it echoed like the distant surging of a muffled sea through the great arena, filtering through wood and steel to where the long line of dressing rooms rested opposite the emergency hospital and the electronic computers of the betting machines. Promoters heard it and grinned over their fat cigars, attendants heard it and grunted as they massaged living flesh, fighters heard it and smiled or frowned according to their temperament. Baron heard it and felt sick.

He sat on a low table, naked but for a pair of shorts, his thick, hair-covered body shining with oil so that his tremendous biceps and thigh muscles gleamed as he shifted with nervous restlessness. To him the roar of the crowd was unclean, as unclean as the simpering women and affected men he had met while with the Eurasian. Memory of them made him draw back his lips in a soundless snarl of contempt and hate. Fools, the lot of them. Blind, senseless fools! And he had catered to their pitiful world of make-believe.

He was glad that he had killed the little brown man.

The door swung open, letting in a screaming roar of animal-like lust, and Hansard slipped into the room. The thin counsellor looked prosperous, his scrawny body covered in sheer synthosilk, rings twinkling on his constantly moving fingers, and the smoke of an expensive cigar curling about his shifting eyes. He slammed the door and grinned at the big man.

'How's it going, Baron? Nervous?'

'Should I be?'

'No. You'll walk over the opposition and tread 'em into the canvas.' He dry-washed his hands. 'We're moving into the big time, Baron. You're the best fighter the Free Circuits have now and if you don't get yourself killed there's no knowing where we'll stop.'

'We?'

'Sure. You, me and Carson.' The shifty eyes narrowed. 'What's the matter?'

'I'm sick of this.' Baron slowly rose from the table. 'I'm tired of having you two scum tell me what to do. I'm tired of going into the ring to beat stupid dolts to a bloody pulp so that perverts can get a cheap, second-hand thrill and you can cash in on the bets. I'm through, Hansard. Finished!'

'Like hell you are!' Savagely the thin man jerked the cigar from his mouth. 'Who took care of you when you killed the Guru? Who wiped your room clear of prints so that the cops couldn't get them? Who hid you out, fed you, supplied all that rotgut you drank? Me and Carson, that's who, and we can turn you in anytime we choose.'

'Can you?' Baron stared at the thin man and his skin glistened as he tensed his muscles. 'Can you?'

'We wouldn't, of course.' Sweat oozed on the thin forehead. 'Take it easy, Baron. You're sick.'

'Yes.' Tiredly the big man slumped back on to the table. 'Yes, I must be. My head — ' He broke off as the thin man produced a bottle. 'Give me that!'

'Steady.' Hansard grunted as the big man snatched it from him, twisted out the cork and gulped the raw spirit as if it had been water. 'Go slow on that stuff. Damn it, man, where do you put it all? I've never seen anyone drink as much as you and still remain above ground. Why do you do it?'

'I don't know.' Baron stared at the half-empty bottle. 'It makes me feel easier, I guess.' He drained the bottle. 'What the hell!'

Sound echoed through the flimsy wall, the roar of the crowd mingled with a harsh, screaming yelling from disappointed customers. Bedlam seemed to have broken out above and men scurried down the corridor as fresh human material went into the ring to quell the incipient riot. Hansard listened to the noise, his eyes flickering over the white-painted room.

'A bad crowd tonight. They want blood and plenty of it. There hadn't been a man killed when I came down, and they don't like it. The promoter had to put a couple on with knives, and even that didn't satisfy them.'

'Why don't they use swords?'

'Rapiers?' The counsellor shook his head. 'It's been tried. Too fast and not enough blood.'

'Not rapiers, swords. Like the Romans did back in the old days?'

'Gladiators?' The thin man licked his lips. 'You've got an idea there. I — ' He broke off as Carson entered the room. 'Say, boss. Baron's come up with a good idea. Why don't we put on a gladiator show? You know what I mean, swords and shields and all that stuff. It should go down well.'

'It might at that.' The hotel owner nodded. 'Could we get material?'

'Sure! I could get any of a dozen who'd put on a show for a thousand credits and the promise of free medical attention.'

'I'll think about it.' Carson jerked his head. 'Get upstairs now and start placing the bets. You know what to do.' He waited until the thin man had left the room, and stared at the big man. 'How do you feel, Baron?'

'Sick as usual. Why?'

'What are you sick about?'

'Don't you know?' Baron flung the empty bottle into a corner. 'You think I like being your trained meal ticket?'

'It feeds you too,' reminded Carson coldly. 'And the way you eat and slop back the liquor makes quite a hole in the bank account.' He smiled and slapped the big man on his oiled shoulder. 'Hell, but you're getting big! Muscle too, real stuff and not this flabby fat most of them have. We'll clean up tonight.'

'Will we?'

'Sure, and then we'll move on. The police were asking after you back at the hotel.'

'Were they?'

'Yes. Asking a lot of peculiar questions. Wanted to know had we noticed any change in you, stuff like that.' He smiled again. 'As if I'd tell them.' His face lost its smile. 'But you have changed. That scar's gone and you're bigger. Your face has altered too, I'd take a bet that your own mother wouldn't recognise you now.'

'Stop it!'

'Hell! I meant no harm.'

'Maybe not, but I don't like that kind of talk.' Baron gripped his temples between his palms and squeezed hard. 'I feel funny, head seems full of mist and I can't think straight.' He glared at the sleek hotel owner. 'Maybe I'm getting punch-drunk.'

'Not you. If you ask me I'd say that rotgut you swallow has something to do with it. You want to take it easy on that stuff.'

'Go to hell!'

Carson shrugged. 'Suit yourself, boy, but you've a hard battle ahead and you've got to win.' He sat on the edge of the table. 'I've put you opposite a real killer. You know the rules, bare handed and nothing barred. Get in there and finish him quick. Don't worry about knocking him out or any stuff like that. There's an ugly crowd upstairs and they're screaming for action. I want you to give it to them.'

'I know what to do.'

'I hope so.' Carson looked up as an attendant stuck his head in at the door. 'Right! We'll be right up.' He looked at Baron. 'Remember now.'

The big man nodded.

The Free Circuits were a product of stifled emotions and a cynical authority. Regulated boxing was too tame to satisfy the customers, and the police worked on the theory that if a man wanted to risk his life and health in the ring he was at liberty to do as he pleased. So the Free Circuits became simulacrums of the ancient arenas, and men, stripped and oiled, fought like wild beasts to the screaming plaudits of a crowd of jaded women and soft-bodied men.

Sometimes men died in the ring, but mostly, however, the combatants took care to cover themselves with blood without serious injury.

Baron stood in his corner and stared at his opponent. A big, hairy, tiny-eyed man faced him, rolls of fat adding weight to a huge body, and his hands opened and closed like the claws of some horrible insect as he shuffled splayed feet in a tray of resin.

'He's a bad one,' whispered Hansard. 'He likes maiming.'

'I've met worse.' Baron sucked air into his lungs and felt his chest expand. Hansard grunted.

'I'm warning you, Baron, Genso is a killer. They've only put him on now to calm down the crowd. Usually he's saved for the big events.'

'I'll handle him,' said Baron, and meant it.

A raucous-voiced man entered the ring and yelled towards a suspended microphone. 'A big event, folks! Genso the Killer against the Cave Man,' he pointed towards Baron. 'A no-rule, no-rest fight to the finish between these perfect specimens of humanity. The winner will be the one remaining on his feet or until the loser admits defeat.' He stepped out of the ring. 'When the bell sounds — attack!'

It was as simple as that.

Baron tensed as the clang of the bell cut over the hum of the crowd. Silence fell as he stepped forward, his shoulders bowed and his head drawn protectively between his shoulders. His chin rested on his chest, his eyes glowering from beneath their heavy arches of bone, and his hands swung almost to his knees as he held them out and forward, the fingers spread to grapple with oiled flesh.

Genso lurched forward with deceptive speed, his huge body quivering with his motion, and Baron shook his head as a fist thudded against his ear. He turned, gripped at an arm and swore as his hands slipped from the oiled skin. Genso laughed and kicked out at Baron.

It was a blow that would have killed an ordinary man and as Baron twisted, the impact of the splayed foot numbed his thigh. He twisted, blocking a savage slash at the nape of his neck, and blinked as stiffened fingers stabbed at his eyes.

They missed, the sharpened fingernails tearing his cheek, and anger came with the blood.

He made a sound deep in his throat, a snarling, animal-like growl, a primitive sound stemming from the fire-lit mist swirling within his skull. Rage flooded through him, dimming his vision and sending the breath whistling through his nostrils. Savagely he lashed out with a knotted fist, feeling it smack against flesh, and he followed up the blow, pounding and pounding at the gross body of the hairy man.

Genso struck back. Coldly, scientifically, sending blood spouting from nostrils and slamming his great hands against the ridge of bone over the eyes. He dodged, aiming at the kidneys, the nape of the neck, driving sledgehammer blows into the sides and stomach of the primitive figure before him. Baron grunted, shaking his head and grabbing at a thrusting arm. His speed surprised the killer. His hands shot out and grabbed at the slick flesh, his thick fingers digging, claw-like in sinew and muscle. Grimly he pulled the gross body towards him.

The crowd roared as they met. A knee stabbed at Baron's groin and he whimpered to the throb of pain. Fingers stabbed again at his eyes as the killer tried his favourite trick of blinding his opponent. Like madmen they fought, like the animals they were, fist and knee, nails and teeth, ripping, tearing, smashing by brute force and surging energy.

Baron snarled as pain stabbed through him and his great hands reached for the killer's throat, his fingers digging into the soft windpipe with irresistible force.

He didn't know just when Genso died, but he did hear the roaring of the crowd.

He shook his head, trying to clear away some of the mist, and dropped the lax figure in his hands as he pressed his palms against his ears to shut out the drumming sound. Money fell around him, and Hansard, his thin face strained and sick, pulled at his arm as he led him towards a corner.

'Baron! Are you all right?'

'What?' Baron swayed as the drumming sound beat around his battered head. 'What's that you say?' The words were thick and guttural in his mouth.

'Snap out of it, man. Here.' The sting of alcohol washed some of the thickness from his throat, and he straightened, blinking as he tried to stare beyond the

175

brilliant circle of light towards the yelling crowd.

'What happened?'

'Don't you know? You killed him, that's what. You beat the Killer. Man, you can ask your own price for a bout after this.'

'Baron!' Carson thrust his way through the crowd surging around the corner. 'Listen. Can you take on a couple more?'

'More?' The big man blinked as he tried to focus the pale face before him. Carson frowned and stared at the counsellor.

'What's the matter with him?'

'Punchy, I guess, or maybe drunk, he doesn't seem to know what he's doing.'

'Good.' Carson smiled. 'I'll fix it so that he takes on a couple of fighters at once then. The promoter will pay fifty thousand for the bout, the crowd's gone wild and he wants to cash in.' He stared at the slumped figure of the big man. 'Do something to get him conscious.'

'He's conscious all right, but Carson,' the thin-faced man wrung his hands. 'Two at once! He won't stand a chance.'

'So what? He's getting to be a

nuisance, just as well if he dies in the ring, and it will get the police off our tail. Forget it.' He smiled and was gone, heading towards the dressing rooms and the waiting promoter. Hansard leaned across the slumped figure hunched on the tiny stool.

'Wake up, Baron! This time you've got a couple of them to face. Snap out of it.' Almost he slapped the heavy features. Almost, but not quite. There was something about the big man, a sense of barely-leashed fury that restrained his hand.

Baron sat and felt his mind dissolve into flame-lit madness. Odours wafted around him, strange and raw, searing his delicate nostrils with warm, animal smells he did not recognise. His ears twitched to the continuous roar of sound and his blood pulsed to anger and fear, throbbing as it raced through his veins and accelerating the pounding of his heart.

Again the raucous-voiced man yelled over the suspended microphone. Again came the tense, anticipatory hush, broken as two men, both big, both well muscled, both sleekly oiled, jumped into the ring. Silence fell with the brazen note of the bell.

Baron rose.

Enemies waited before him. Strangers from some other tribe, and he roared his challenge as he shambled towards them, his knotted fists pounding at the barrel of his chest. He roared and pounded, froth spewing from his writhing lips, his head sunk between his shoulders, his eyes glowing coals as they peered from beneath his shaggy brows. For a long moment he stood there, proud of his vibrant strength, sending the dull echoes of his beaten chest throbbing over the amplifiers, his snarling challenge harsh and heavy with the sense of things and places long dead.

It startled them. It sent strange pricklings running up their spines. It held them immobile with the utter inconsistency of his actions and, before they could recover, Baron had flung himself forward in a battering fury of bone and muscle. A skull crunched beneath his swinging fist, and he caught the sagging body, lifting it high above his head and flinging it at the remaining fighter. Dodging, the man found himself in a grip of steel and he shrieked as he felt himself being lifted, and screamed again as he was flung from the ring, hurtling through the air to collapse in a lifeless heap as he smashed against a row of pale faces.

In the empty ring Baron roared with savage triumph at the destruction of his enemies.

'Carson!' The fat promoter wiped sweat from his flabby jowls. 'That boy of yours, can he take on more?'

'Why not?' The sleek man licked his lips as he stared at the distant ring where a solitary figure stalked like a figment of a forgotten dream. 'Pay?'

'I'd like to send them in until he's beaten. Fifty thousand?'

'Make it a hundred and you can do as you like.' Carson grinned as he listened to the crowd. 'Get that? They're almost crazy out there. Send your boys round for extra cash and send in a couple more. If they flop try it with three and then three again. Baron's big, but he can't last out forever.'

'They'll kill him.'

'So what? A hundred thousand?'

'Yeah.' The promoter turned to relay swift orders, and Carson edged nearer to the ringside to see the fun. The crowd was silent now, listening to the blur of sound from the speakers as the announcer yelled into the microphone, and men moved between the hushed rows collecting money from the eager patrons. In the ring Baron had stopped moving about and sat, head bowed, on a small stool in his corner. Hansard leaned over him, whispering, his thin features ghastly in their pallor.

'This is it, Baron. Two more and then three if you last.' He swallowed as he looked at the bowed shape. 'Can you hear me? They're going to kill you, tear you to pieces for the mob, do you know that?' He dabbed at his streaming forehead. 'God! I didn't know it would be like this.' He jerked as men slipped into the ring and the bell sounded its brazen note. 'On your feet, Baron. This is it!'

Baron didn't move.

He sat, shoulders bowed and head lowered, and within him surged a dreadful terror. Dimly, fighting vast tides of black emotion, his intelligence flickered like a dying star.

The rage had passed, the blood-fury, and now he sat and trembled as he felt his mind totter on the edge of irrevocable oblivion. The past few minutes were a blur, an impression of possession, as if someone or something else had taken over his body and mind. He had the horrible fear that, mentally at least, he was going to die.

One of the fighters, playing for a cheer, cocky in his vibrant fitness and contempt for all lesser men, danced forward and smashed his fist like a club down on the sunken head.

Fire exploded within the thickened skull. A surging wash of searing brilliance, and against it the dying flicker of intelligence vanished like a blown candle. Baron snarled, air whistling through his flared nostrils as he caught an alien scent and, as the fist descended again, he caught it with a bone-snapping grip.

He rose, still gripping the broken wrist, and biceps and pectorals writhed beneath his oiled, hair-matted skin. He spun and, like a shrieking doll, the trapped fighter spun with him, his feet leaving the sleazy canvas of the ring, whirling in a circle, once, twice, then, as Baron released his hold, hurtling towards the other man. Flesh smacked against flesh. Before the fallen man could struggle to his feet Baron had jumped forward, leaping high into the air and coming down with terrible force on top of the half-stunned fighter.

The crowd shrieked. A surging wash of roaring sound, and as other men, not so cocky now and moving with nervous caution, slipped into the ring the pounding roar became a throbbing chant.

'*Kill! Kill! Kill!*'

It turned Baron into the beast he had become. He roared as he saw fresh enemies and the deep booming of his beaten chest sounded like the pounding of a primordial drum. Turning, he gripped one of the ring posts, wrenching it from its socket and tearing free the hampering ropes. Like a club he swung it, a ponderous mass of wood and metal, whining as it cut through the smoke-filled air.

The fighters ran. They spun and raced from the terrible monstrosity behind them, jumping from the ring and down into the crowd, their nerves broken by something they could not even begin to understand. Others joined them, those well-dressed men and women who had paid highly for the ringside seats so as to get a good view of the fighting. They rose and fought among themselves as they ran from the snarling, roaring thing behind them.

Baron followed them.

He grunted as he swung the improvised club. Within seconds the great arena became a bedlam of screaming women and shouting men, all fighting desperately to escape the terrible, blood-splashed figure who, a moment before, they had been urging to destruction.

Through them, swinging the post like a flail, Baron moved towards the dressing rooms and the exit.

Suddenly the way before him was clear, the frantic crowd had forced itself from his path, and he lunged forward, his sunken eyes red as they peered from their bone-ridged sockets.

Forward and out — into the ruins of the old city.

10

A monster walked the streets of Greater New York. Whitney sat in McMillan's office and read the sheaf of reports, half listening to the droning voice from a wall-speaker as he scanned the closely-typed columns.

'Woman reported that a strange man accosted her. Man states that his fruit shop was robbed by an ape. A couple felt eyes watching them and saw a giant monkey squatting on a wall. Two-liquor shops raided and their proprietors killed. A man found dead, neck broken, his bag of shopping empty by his side. A police officer shot at a dim shape that refused to halt when commanded. A drunk swore that he had seen a gorilla — '

Whitney sighed as he dropped the sheaf and listened to the droning voice. It was from the mobile patrol centre, and the young man frowned as he listened to the words.

185

'Are you sure that your men under-stand?' He looked accusingly at the inspector. 'No shooting unless in self-defence.'

'I've told them what to do.' McMillan grunted as he examined a map and moved pins to correspond with the positions of the searching patrols. 'They will move in and surround him, then notify us where he is.'

'He mustn't be killed.' Whitney rose to his feet and began to pace about the small office. 'From the reports it is obvious that the retrogression has progressed beyond anything we dreamed about. Baron is no longer quite human. His intelligence must have been submerged by the primitive instincts and he must be in a state bordering on complete terror.'

'Yeah?' McMillan shrugged. 'From the way he acted at the arena I wouldn't have thought so.'

'The arena!' For a moment it seemed almost as if the young doctor would spit. 'Isn't it about time you closed down the Free Circuits?'

'Why should we? If they want to rip

each other apart, then let them, they'd do it anyway, and it keeps regulated boxing clean.'

'Turning men into beasts and watching them maim and kill each other.' Whitney shrugged. 'What happened was poetic justice, you can't blame Baron for what they did to him.'

'I'm not blaming him at all.' McMillan stared at the young man. 'Anyway, it happened two weeks ago, and I've got other worries. The thing is that Baron killed more than twenty people and over a hundred others were trampled to death in the rush to escape.' He frowned. 'If Carson and that other man, Hansard I think it was, hadn't died we may have got some important information. I'd still like to know just how Baron managed to escape observation for so long. From what I hear Baron didn't even look human then.'

'Do any of those fighters?' Whitney shrugged. 'They probably shaved him and disguised him as much as they could. Not that anyone would bother in the Free Circuits. The man was a fighter and good for a show, and the more animal he looked the better they would like it. It's the present I'm worried about, not the past.'

'We'll get him,' said McMillan calmly. 'I've got every man on the force combing the ruins, they're bound to flush him out and corner him.'

'Did you try the bait as I suggested?'

'We did. Baskets of fruit, all nicely drugged, placed about the areas where he had been reported. Not one of them has been touched, but the robberies and killings still go on.' The inspector rifled a sheaf of reports. 'He seems to have concentrated on the butcher shops lately, and there are quite a few dogs and cats missing. Would he be changing his diet?'

'Man is an omnivorous animal, he can live on both meat and vegetables, but our very early ancestors were hunters, not farmers.'

'Should we try drugged meat as bait then?'

'No. He can probably sense there is something wrong, perhaps even smell the odour of the drug or the men who handled it. Don't forget that his senses are far sharper than ours, smell, vision, hearing even. They had to be for man to survive at all back in the prehistoric age.'

'You know,' said McMillan thoughtfully, 'the more I think about what you told me the more fantastic it seems. Here we have Baron, a civilised man, a space pilot, turning into a thing like that. I can accept the theory, I've seen too much to be dogmatic about anything, but that a civilised, cultured man should revert back to a gorilla-like ape-man. It doesn't seem to make sense.'

'It's a fact.' Whitney listened to the droning voice from the wall-speaker and slumped down into a chair. 'The alcohol started it, and then the radiations from the sludge pits, God knows what they did to his metabolism and mind. Then just to make it worse they had to make a fighter out of him. They deliberately put him in the very circumstances where he had to depend on killer instinct and brute force.' He gritted his teeth. 'They deserved everything he did to them.'

'Would it have been any different if you

had taken him in charge?'

'Yes. We could have plotted his physical structure change and by mental therapy kept a residue of his conscious mind in control. With drugs and neuron surgery we may even have been able to check the retrogression, but in any case he would have had scientific care and release from all pleasure.' He stared sombrely at the inspector. 'Think of what we could have learned. The shift in some of the internal organs, the alteration in bone structure, the difference in the glands. We could have traced evolution back over half a million years and answered for all time just how we became to be what we are. We may have discovered just what is the purpose of the pineal gland, the vestigial 'third eye' within the skull. We could have traced the evolutionary life of the appendix and found out just how intelligent our ancestors were. So many questions, and instead of that — '

He broke of as the voice echoed with new urgency from the wall-speaker.

'Central Office. We have found the ape-man.'

'Where?' McMillan threw a switch connecting him to the mobile patrol centre.

'Among the ruins, East Side, north from the river. Shall we go in?'

'No. Wait until I get there.' McMillan rose from his desk. 'Coming?'

'You couldn't stop me,' said Whitney. He ran after the policeman and dived into the waiting turbo-car.

The drive was a short one, but to the impatient doctor it seemed to take forever. He stared at the bleak ruins of the waterfront, rotten with decay and abandoned as the city pushed out to the spaceport. Before them the headlights of the car shone on a group of armed, uniformed men.

'McMillan.' The inspector identified himself. 'Where is he?'

'Just beyond the ruined warehouse. We spotted him about a mile away and tracked him down.'

'Dogs?'

'Yes, sir.' The man hesitated. 'They tracked him but refused to go any further. Shall we — '

'Get rid of the dogs,' snapped Whitney. 'They will only frighten him. Take them back to their kennels, we don't want even their scent hanging around.'

'Do as he says,' ordered the inspector. He looked at the young man. 'Any ideas?'

'I suppose that your men have surrounded the area?'

'Naturally.'

'Are they sure about their orders? No shooting unless absolutely necessary. I don't want some trigger-happy fool cutting loose just for the fun of it.'

'They know what to do.' McMillan stepped from the car and stared towards the dim shape of the ruined building. 'A pity that it isn't daylight, but we'll have to make out with searchlights. Tear gas?'

'Yes, sir.'

'Good. Then close in. Slowly and don't make too much noise. Cut off the building from the rest of the city. Have plenty of lights to both sides and rear and issue gas weapons. Any man shooting without justification will be answerable to me.'

'What do you intend doing?' Whitney

glanced at the men around him, moving with quiet efficiency as they carried out the inspector's orders. 'Remember, I don't want him harmed.'

'We'll do the best we can,' promised McMillan, 'but I can't promise anything. You seem to forget that there is a murderer in there. I can't ask my men to let him kill a few of them just to preserve an interesting laboratory specimen. If they are attacked they will have the right to shoot.' He glanced up at the dark building. 'Once the sides and back are covered with lights we'll move in. I'm trusting that he will be more afraid of the searchlights than of us. Once we know just where he is the tear gas can be used to either knock him out or drive him from cover.'

'What then?'

'We've got some nets handy and a few men who have had experience in capturing wild animals. If nothing goes wrong we'll have Baron nicely wrapped and ready for delivery before the morning.' He turned to an officer. 'Sides and back covered?'

'Yes, sir.'

'Right. Lights.'

Fingers of stabbing brilliance streamed from the projectors while other lights, broadened and dispersed, bathed the sides and back of the ruin with floodlit splendour.

'See anything?'

'Not yet, sir.' The officer sent a beam of light stabbing into the dark opening of windows. 'I thought that if we filled the upper section with gas we might drive him down.'

'Good idea. Do it.'

Whitney flinched to the thud of guns, and tear gas shells spat from the squat, wide-muzzled weapons and arched towards the gaping windows. They exploded with muffled roars, and a thick white cloud of released gas trickled over the face of the building as it streamed from the upper stories.

'More gas, sir?'

'Wait a bit.' McMillan stared at the young doctor. 'Any idea how he may react if we went inside?'

'It wouldn't be too healthy. He is

frightened and confused and the only way he knows how to react is by force. It is the only way he can react. The primitive reflex, in fact the only one in the early days, was to destroy everything and anything that threatened. The idea of gods and superstitions came much later in the evolutionary scale, and treating with your enemies later still. Charity and trust are almost modern concepts.'

'So you advise against it.' McMillan frowned at the drifting clouds of gas. 'I don't want to fill the building if I can help it. If I do we'll have to use masks and they are cumbersome. I suppose that it's even possible the gas wouldn't affect him?'

'To a lesser degree, perhaps, but I wouldn't like to be positive about that.' He looked at the drifting beams of light. 'There might be just one way. If I could appeal to his intelligence he may listen to me.'

'Listen? But I thought you said his intelligence had vanished?'

'Not vanished. It couldn't do that. Just submerged by his subconscious instincts. There may be just a possibility that I could awaken his awareness, his ego, and that he would respond enough for us to capture him without harm. Have you a loudhailer?'

'Yes.'

'Then if I could use it?'

McMillan nodded and turned to issue the order. He spun as one of the searchlights died with a dull report and a shower of glass. 'What the hell?'

'He's throwing things, sir.' The man ducked as something hurled towards them and smashed against the housing of the light. 'I caught a glimpse of a face at one of the lower windows.'

'Down!' McMillan swore as something hummed through the air above his head and a man cried out with the pain of a broken arm. 'Take cover!'

More missiles followed, hurled with incredible force, slamming against the metal of cars and equipment, smashing the lenses of the searchlights and spraying the crouching men with splinters of broken rubble.

'Bricks!' The inspector cringed as one exploded, bomb-like, a few feet from his face. 'He's bombarding us with bricks!'

'It's the lights,' explained Whitney. 'The beams frightened him, he probably thinks that they are the eyes of some monster. Let me call to him.'

'Where in hell is that loudhailer?' The inspector inched backwards and behind the shelter of a turbo-car. 'Pass it over. Quick!' He handed the instrument to the young doctor. 'Here. Just press this button and speak into the mike.'

Whitney nodded, inched himself forward so that he could see the building, and waited until the last of the searchlights died as McMillan ordered them to be cut. He pressed the button.

'Baron!' His amplified voice thundered from the shell of the building, echoing over the ruins and bringing a sudden hush. 'Baron. Answer me, Baron. Baron.' Grimly he repeated the name, trying to arouse individual awareness in the creature lurking among the ruins. 'Baron!'

He released the button and in the following silence little sounds became remarkably loud. The shuffle of feet, the sound of a man coughing and of another nervously working the bolt of his sub-gun. Beside him McMillan breathed quiet orders and men moved into position armed with nets and gas rifles.

'Baron!' Again the huge voice roared against the silence. 'Bar — ' Something whined through the air and smashed against the metal and plastic instrument. Whitney grunted, almost stunned, and spat a mouthful of blood and broken teeth.

'What happened?' McMillan stared at the young man.

'He threw a brick.' Whitney dabbed at his injured mouth. 'If it hadn't hit the amplifier it would have torn my head off.' He ducked as another missile clanged against the side of the car. 'This is getting us nowhere. I'm going in.'

'You're what!'

'Going in after him. Get me something to use as a gift, a basket of fruit will do or a lump of meat.' He nursed his aching mouth. 'And while you're at it get me a shot of novocaine or cocaine. These broken teeth are giving me hell.'

'I don't like it.' McMillan shook his

head. 'You're crazy even to think of it.'

'No I'm not. The loudhailer frightened him as the searchlights did. He probably thought that the lights were the eyes and the amplified voice its roar. If I walk in alone and with a gift, he might not attack. After all he must be starving by now; with his increased metabolism he needs a lot of food, and he may decide to eat first and act afterwards.' Whitney grunted at the pain in his lacerated mouth. 'Anyway, it's worth a try. I don't want him injured or shocked any more than I can help. Scientifically, Baron is the most valuable thing in the entire Solar System — and I want to keep him that way.'

'If you think it's worth the chance — ' The inspector gave rapid orders instructing his men to fetch meat and drugs. 'I'll order complete silence while you're making the attempt, but you'll be covered and any move attacking you will be the signal for a blast of fire. Here.' He passed over a compact medical kit and watched as the young doctor numbed the nerves of his face. 'Here is the meat, fresh from a butcher's shop, and undrugged. Anything else?'

'No lights. No noise. And no shooting.' Whitney rose to his feet, the raw meat in his hands. 'Wish me luck.'

Slowly he began to walk towards the building.

It was dark and silent and he seemed to be walking over a pit of shadows. Even though he knew that he was circled with watching men yet he felt utterly alone and he had to fight against the instinctive desire to drop everything and run, and run, and keep on running back to the calm normalcy of the Luna Laboratories and the society of old friends.

He kept on walking.

Before him the ruined building loomed high and black against the stars, a thin nimbus of light seeping from its rear as the floodlights destroyed the darkness with their man-made brilliance. Eyes stared at him, the watchful eyes of civilised men crouched behind their guns, and other eyes, small and sunken, peering from beneath lowering brows as they stared at this strange animal walking with fresh meat in its hands. Meat that Baron must desperately need. Food to fill the empty belly, to supply energy for the speeded metabolism, food for a starving primitive whose only instinct was to eat when he had to, and kill when hungry.

And Baron was starving.

Nearer to the looming building. Nearer, and every moment Whitney imagined a hairy arm sweeping back and a brick, the modern equivalent of a jagged-edged flint, hurling towards him with incredible force. Grimly he strode forward, his throat dry and his mangled mouth tense as he forced quivering nerves and rebelling muscles to carry him nearer to the waiting creature before him.

'Baron!' He spoke quietly, the sound of his voice startlingly loud in the silence. 'Baron.' He raised the blood-dripping meat. 'Baron. I am your friend. I bring food! Food! Food!' He fell silent, his legs still carrying him forward, and from one of the watching men, it may have been the inspector, came a muffled curse.

'Baron!' Now he was almost up to the

building. 'Baron! Food!'

Something stirred in the shadows.

'Baron!' Sweat oozed from his forehead, but Whitney forced himself to step even nearer. 'Food.'

He halted then, slowly bending down to place the meat on the ground and slowly straightening. He trembled, almost lost in primitive fear of the unnatural, but his coldly calculating scientific training made him move with cautious precision. He stepped back, still facing the dim shape in the shadows, and his hands moved slowly from his own body to the meat, from the meat to the almost invisible creature staring at him, from the creature back to the meat.

Baron stepped forward.

Even though he had known what to expect, Whitney felt incredible disbelief. It didn't seem possible that a man could have altered so much, and he stared at the dim shape limned by the seeping light from the rear of the building, his eyes wide as they tried to take in every detail at once.

Hair, of course, a thick mat of it over

the body and face, leaving only the eyes and ears, nostrils and mouth free. The forehead sloped backwards, the jaw was tremendous and the canines showed white as they rested on the lower lip. From sloping shoulders, bowed with their burden of muscle, long arms hung level with the knees. The thighs were massive, bowed a little, matching the calves and splayed feet. The stomach and waist were thick, slabbed with muscle and fat, and the chest was a tremendous barrel-shaped thing, so big that the arms hung forward and out as the creature shambled forward.

It was armed. A great mass of concrete pierced with a length of twisted iron, rusty now and stained with damp, obviously fallen from a collapsing wall, but serving as a potent club. Whitney licked his lips as he saw it, noting the weight and the ease with which it was carried. One blow from that crude weapon and his head would be driven down into his chest, his torso smashed down to his knees.

Baron stared at the meat, stared at the

man, and the great club swung upwards as the lips writhed back from the teeth.

Light blazed from the watching men. A stabbing finger of brilliance striking from the projector and playing full on the brutish features.

'Cut the light!' Whitney swore with helpless anger. 'It was a gesture, a warning, nothing to worry about. Cut that damned light!'

He was too late. Baron snarled and the great club swung up in the massive fist. He roared and with the sound something of the long-dead past touched the watching men, something primeval and long buried, some response to a forgotten threat and oddly familiar challenge. One man felt it a little more than the others. One man's instincts writhed his lips back in a soundless snarl, forced his eyes to blaze hate as they sighted along the barrel of his weapon, tightened his finger on the curved metal of the trigger.

The stutter of the sub-gun came just as the massive club was about to descend. Red blossoms flowered in a ragged line across the barrel-chest. Lead whined in a lethal stream as it spread towards the staggering figure, smashing through skin and muscle, bone and sinew, tearing into vitals and blasting the life from a thing that should never have lived. Whitney sobbed with frustrated rage as the descending club, falling by its own weight, brushed his shoulder and sent him, bruised and numb, to the debris-littered ground. He jerked to his feet just as the snarl of the sub-gun faded into shocked silence.

Grimly he stared down at the thing at his feet. Dead now. The strange metabolism had converted a normal body into the one which had walked the Earth a half million years ago stilled by the pounding impact of hot lead. The accidental miracle that could have answered so many questions, solved so many problems, ended forever. Looking down at the dead thing Whitney felt a great sadness and a great shame. He had done this. Science had done it, acting like God and restoring the dead to a life, which, though brief, must have been worse than any hell. He remembered Baron's bitter scorn at the double-edged gift of being allowed to die twice,

We do hope that you have enjoyed reading this large print book.

Did you know that all of our titles are available for purchase?

We publish a wide range of high quality large print books including:

Romances, Mysteries, Classics
General Fiction
Non Fiction and Westerns

Special interest titles available in large print are:

The Little Oxford Dictionary
Music Book, Song Book
Hymn Book, Service Book

Also available from us courtesy of Oxford University Press:

Young Readers' Dictionary
(large print edition)
Young Readers' Thesaurus
(large print edition)

For further information or a free brochure, please contact us at:

Ulverscroft Large Print Books Ltd.,
The Green, Bradgate Road, Anstey,
Leicester, LE7 7FU, England.
Tel: (00 44) 0116 236 4325
Fax: (00 44) 0116 234 0205

RAT RUN

Frederick Nolan

Her Majesty's Secret Service agent Garrett, investigating a series of suicides by scientific researchers, discovers the parameters of a cataclysmic terrorist strike. The fanatical André Dur puts his unholy scenario into operation over the geological fault called the 'Rat Run', where nuclear submarines stalk each other in the dark depths. Helplessly the world looks on as the minutes tick away. Garrett's desperate mission is to neutralise Dur's deadly countdown — the ultimate ecological disaster, Chernobyl on the high seas.

THE SECRET AGENT

Rafe McGregor

Two days after September 11, 2001, an intelligence officer from the South African Secret Service arrived in Washington, D.C. Three months later he was responsible for the arrest of Richard Reid, the notorious British *al-Qaeda* operative . . . A series of short stories follow secret agent Jackson from Boston to Oxford, Quebec City, the Italian Alps, and his final and most deadly mission four months after his premature retirement.

THE PRICE OF FREEDOM

E. C. Tubb

When his wife is murdered, the victim of an assassin's bullet, businessman Dell Weston soon finds his life is falling apart. Betrayed by his partner, he loses control of his company, and descends into the lower strata of a dog-eat-dog society. Somehow, Dell manages to survive long enough to question the very fabric of civilisation — and the role played by the mysterious figures in grey — the Arbitrators . . .